THIS , Song's FOR YOU

AMIE TEMPLETON

LitPrime Solutions
21250 Hawthorne Blvd
Suite 500, Torrance, CA 90503
www.litprime.com
Phone: 1 (209) 788-3500

Published by LitPrime Solutions   12/04/2020

ISBN: 978-1-953397-29-4(sc)
ISBN: 978-1-953397-30-0(e)

Library of Congress Control Number: 2020923153

Contents

Preface v

Introduction vii

Chapter 1 1

Chapter 2 5

Chapter 3 10

Chapter 4 16

Chapter 5 21

Chapter 6 29

Chapter 7 36

Chapter 8 40

Chapter 9 46

Chapter 10 53

Chapter 11 57

Chapter 12 62

Chapter 13 67

Chapter 14 76

Chapter 15 82

Chapter 16 86

Chapter 17 89

Chapter 18 94

Chapter 19 100

Chapter 20 106

Chapter 21 112

Chapter 22 120

Chapter 23 126

Chapter 24 135

Chapter 25 140

Chapter 26 147

Chapter 27 156

Preface

Any trauma has the potential to impact on one's family. In my case, I learnt the hard way that it was wise to tread lightly.

I am grateful that my husband John and I have developed a mutual respect over the years, although in earlier times it was hard to accept that it was as much John's right not to show interest in my spiritual quest as it was my right to follow my heart.

It would have been easy for us to go our separate ways, but instead we chose to walk parallel paths for quite a few years. Much later, John came to respect what I was doing and now he good-naturedly calls me a spook, which I accept as a term of endearment.

I have taken the title of this book from a song Wayne wrote for me and my reason is twofold. Firstly, he is part of this story and I believe his death was meant as my wake-up call. Secondly, I have used the word 'song' as a metaphor for 'message' to all who read the book.

I am now fulfilled by sharing in the running of a weekly meditation group and participating in healings for its members. In my daily life I am of service by doing my best to live what I have learnt, and by helping out in whichever area I am asked or feel the call.

Introduction

In 1982 my nineteen-year-old son Wayne was found murdered and my life changed forever. The trauma I experienced forced me to question the very depth of my existence.

I embarked on a search to find the answers and my quest led me through a maze of information and advice, but for a long time the answers I found simply created more questions. Progress was slow and I met with much disappointment and frustration, mainly because it is in my nature to have everything cut and dried – right *now*. It was difficult to learn patience. Trust was also an important issue and countless times I either ignored or refused to accept the truth even when it was right in front of me.

Not too many years ago it was taboo to speak openly of a psychic or spiritual experience, but thankfully great progress has been made towards freedom of discussion in these areas. In 1982 I met with ridicule for following a path that differed from general belief. Naivety led me to share certain experiences, but I soon learnt to be more discreet when in the company of those who might misunderstand my interests.

Today there is no real need for secrecy and help is easy to find. However, I believe there are still many people who are searching for answers. They might not know where to look for help and perhaps feel, as I did, that they are alone with their dilemma. I hope the story of my search, and where it led me, will be of help to such people.

Each step of my journey took me closer to the discovery that we are more than a physical body; that we are never alone; and that help is there for the asking. Even though the pathways might differ for each person, every signpost ultimately guides all seekers to the same place – themselves.

Amie Templeton.

Chapter 1

One night in November 1981, I was alone watching television when, for no apparent reason, a strange unrest came over me. I shuddered, and became fearful as sensations filled my head. There were no words, just a knowing with absolute certainty that someone near to mewas soon going to die.

I covered my ears in shock as if to block the source of these terrifying feelings and paced from room to room trying to focus my thoughts. At forty-one I had not lost anyone close. My grandparents and father had died but I believed that was the nature of things.

I pictured my two brothers Eric and Alan and two sisters Maree and Sonya, who all lived in the Eastern States, and tried to imagine life without them. Then I thought of my immediate family here in Perth – and went cold. As I went through them one by one – my husband John, a long- distance truck driver, and sons Matthew, Neil and Wayne my head screamed, 'No! Not one of them! How could I part with any one of them?'

The intensity of the episode subsided over the next hour or two, but I couldn't forget it. Although I hid behind a smiling face when John and the boys were home, I felt anything but happy. I wanted to tell them what I knew so we could work together to avert the disaster I could see approaching. But how could I explain *how* I knew

---

[1] There are no unnatural or supernatural phenomena, only very large gaps in our knowledge of what is natural. We should strive to fill those gaps of ignorance,' said Apollo 14 Astronaut Edgar Mitchell, founder of the Institute of Noetic Science (IONS.)

I was constantly crying for no reason and plagued by depression. I could barely concentrate on everyday chores nothing seemed important any more. I had no idea where to reach for help, and became nervous and withdrawn.

But life moved on and just after Christmas we bought a house in another suburb of Perth. I was still tidying up after the move and decided to go through a box of odds and ends left in the garage by previous owners. I took my time sorting the contents, idly tossing old books and magazines towards a pile destined for the rubbish bin. As one dog- eared magazine left my hands, familiar words on the cover caught my eye. I walked over and picked it up and stared in disbelief at the bold print, 'THE MURDER OF WAYNE TEMPLETON.'

I dropped the magazine and gasped, "Oh, dear God!"

After a few seconds, I picked it up and looked again at the title, realizing this time that it actually read 'THE MURDER OF ROBBIE McWAYNE.'

But it was too late. That first rush of panic had filled my entire body, and now every shaking part of me knew I had just received unmistakable confirmation of impending tragedy.

Wayne was loving and spontaneous and never baulked at giving me a hug and kiss, even in front of his friends. He played the drums and loved his music, waking up many nights to scribble down lyrics that were running through his head. When he was fifteen, he wrote me a song he called 'Mum This Song's For You' and gave me a taped copy. We knew it wasn't destined to make the top ten, but it had a very special place in my heart.

This is part of that song.

I'd like to have a limousine, a mansion on a hill

I'd like to be a millionaire though I probably never will

But if ever I could have one wish I'll tell you what I'd do

I'd wish that every kid could have a mum as great as you.

So mum this song's for you

I'm sorry it's all I can give you

But it's something that's come

Straight from my heart.

Mum this song's for you

Mum I'll always love you

There's nothing that could

Break us two apart.

He liked the girls, but it wasn't until now, at nineteen, that he met Carol who was just eighteen, and formed his first serious relationship. They were planning their engagement later in the year and I often smiled to myself as I watched the two of them together, for they looked to be really in love.

Early in January 1982, when my mother came from Sydney for a visit, Wayne was more than happy to offer her his room, and went to stay at Carol's place which she shared with her friends Donna and Jim.

One evening, about a week later, the phone rang.

"Mrs. Templeton, Wayne and Jim haven't come home. I'm getting worried not knowing where they are."

I swallowed, and then found my voice. "Where did they go, Carol? When were they supposed to be back?"

"They went to Pemberton last Friday in a car Wayne borrowed from your friend Walter at the car yard," she said. "And Wayne called on Saturday, and said they'd be home the next day."

Before we hung up I said calmly, "Don't worry Carol, I'll see what I can find out." But the sick feeling in the pit of my stomach belied any confidence I might have conveyed. It was Tuesday, which meant a few days had passed with no word. Wayne always phoned when he unexpectedly stayed out – even for one night. He called either at night or very early the next morning, knowing I would worry if he didn't let me know he was okay. There was no reason to think he would change this habit, so I knew he or Jim would have called Carol or me if they'd been delayed – that is, unless something had prevented them from doing so.

Chapter 2

John, Neil and mum were having a lively conversation in the lounge room and when they didn't stop talking at my first attempt to attract their attention, I shouted over the top of them, "Please keep quiet for a minute!"

I ignored their irritation as they turned to look at me. My heart thundered and my voice trembled, yet the words came out quietly. "Wayne and Jim are missing. Carol rang and said they should have been home two days ago. Does anyone know where they might have gone?"

During the weeks that passed we called every person even remotely connected to Wayne, but nobody had heard from him or knew where he was. We rang Walter at the car yard to apologise and to get the details of the car. Then we put an advertisement in a Pemberton newspaper giving the plate number and other details, hoping someone in that town might be able to help.

After anxious days with no replies, we knew it was time to admit something was seriously wrong. The following morning, with John away up north, Matthew accompanied Carol and me to Police Headquarters in Perth to file a missing persons report.

We answered questions about Wayne's name and address, but when it came to his age, the police officer put his pen down on the desk.

"Lots of people go missing at that age," he said, "but they usually turn up when they're ready. Then all this paperwork's for nothing, and we've wasted our valuable time."

We tried to convince him that this was not the case with Wayne, and that he would not just disappear and cause us this agony.

"The car he was driving was borrowed from friends of ours at a sales yard, and he'd never let them down either," I added.

The officer was unmoved, so I continued, my voice rising a notch, "He was going to buy the car when he came back. He wouldn't have just run off!"

Then Matthew said firmly, "Look, he's my brother. He wouldn't stay away without letting us know where he is! It's just not like him!"

With a sigh, the officer picked up his pen and completed the form.

* * *

On the morning of St. Patrick's Day, 17th March, 1982, I saw Wayne surrounded by dirt and trees. I was awake in bed, looking at a scene that was only in my head. Wayne was lying still and wore a shirt with a printed pattern, and brown trousers. A creek or river ran behind him not far away.

That was the day the police found the car. It had apparently been abandoned for some time, in the car park of a suburban Perth hotel. Nobody could explain how the car came to be there and the police inquiry was immediately intensified.

The days dragged on and then, on 26th March 1982, exactly two months after the boys disappeared, two solemn police officers came to the front door. They delivered the grim news that the bodies of Wayne and Jim had been found buried on a farm in Pemberton and that a man had confessed to both murders.

The afternoon newspaper's headlines blazed, 'TEENAGERS AXED TO DEATH,' and 'BODIES FOUND IN BUSH GRAVE' and the television news was full of every shocking detail. The reports said that the murderer – Dennis Nosworthy – killed Wayne and Jim while they were asleep. He then covered them with plastic bags, buried them about thirty metres from the house and planted sweet corn over their graves. He also admitted driving Wayne's car to Perth as a decoy.

Giving a motive for his actions, Nosworthy said he believed the boys had come to steal his marihuana crop. However, Nosworthy's brother Jason told reporters that Nosworthy was known for his rages and that in his opinion Wayne and Jim were just in the wrong place at the wrong time. I doubt that the truth will ever be known.

Our telephone rang continuously and the news reports were endless. I remember that at some stage, and for reasons that could not be explained, our television and telephone went dead in the same minute and remained out of commission for twenty-four-hours. We accepted the silence as a form of respite from our ordeal.

When I was asked to identify Wayne's clothes at police headquarters several days later, I was only slightly surprised to find that they were the same shirt and trousers he had been wearing in my 'vision'. And when detectives showed me a map of the place where the boys were found, it was no surprise at all to see a river running through the area.

Wayne and Jim's funerals were held the same day. almost a week later. Most of our relatives came from Queensland, New South Wales and Canberra to support us, and Jim's parents came from Melbourne. I was numb all the while, as though in some kind of dream and I'm sure I didn't communicate any depth of emotion – it was locked inside. John, Matthew and Neil didn't seem able to talk about their feelings either and so we each dealt with the pain in our own way.

Sadly for us, Carol and Donna, severely traumatised, went home to their families in Melbourne and Queensland two weeks after the funeral. My mother stayed on to help where possible before reluctantly returning to Sydney.

* * *

One night when John was away, depressed and unable to sleep, I went to the lounge room and lit a cigarette. Then, with the volume very low so I wouldn't wake the boys, I played Wayne's song over and over trying to dispel my misery. Instead of helping, the lyrics had the opposite effect of making me feel more miserable and soon I was drowning in tears of self-pity.

I poured myself a brandy, mechanically added some coke, and drank it down. It was more brandy than coke and made me cough, but it also made me feel good so I mixed another. Somewhere during the third drink – or it might have been the fourth – the walls didn't look straight, but I lit another cigarette and played the song yet again.

At daybreak I woke up on the lounge with a throbbing headache and feeling very ill. An unfinished drink sat on the coffee table and a dead cigarette end still dangled from my fingers. I lurched down the hall and was violently ill in the toilet. Disgusted with myself, I vowed never again to over-indulge. I edged along the wall to the bathroom and looked in the mirror. Two swollen bloodshot eyes stared back at me from a red, puffy face and my hair was a matted mess. A horrible sight. As I reached for my toothbrush I noticed, for the first time, that Wayne's spare toothbrush was still in the holder on the wall.

Chapter 3

The grief was unrelenting, and in my mind it set me apart from most people. Everywhere I went, I felt that those I passed on the street or saw in the shops could see right inside me; could see my open wound; could see where part of my heart was missing. At first I felt compelled to tell people – even those I hardly knew – what had happened, whether they wanted to hear it or not. But as weeks passed, this stage of grief changed, and if I recognized a person walking towards me, I crossed the street to deliberately avoid contact with them. It was with enormous difficulty that I tried to move on with my life.

About three months after Wayne's funeral, while shopping at a market I found a stack of second-hand books going cheap. One that attracted my attention was *Voices in My Ear* by Doris Stokes and a quick perusal told me this lady could communicate with the dead, so I bought the book out of curiosity.

Stokes claimed that people didn't actually die, and this concept touched me deeply. There was so much to learn about the complexity of life; so many questions I wanted answered. For instance, how could I have known that someone close to me would die? How was it that only weeks before Wayne's disappearance I saw a magazine with his name in reverse? And how could I have known what the area looked like where he was buried, or what clothes he was wearing when he went missing? It was all a profound mystery to me, and I had to know more.

I didn't know where to buy other books like *Voices in My Ear*, nor did I know anyone I could ask. Did such books *have* a genre? If so, what was it? Psychology? Science? Afraid of being laughed at if I asked for help, I scoured the shelves of bookshops in several suburbs, but found nothing.

On my way out of the door of the last shop on my list I saw a notice board, and with nothing else to do, stopped to read the different attached leaflets and brochures. When I came to one that advertised psychic readings, I rummaged in my bag for a pen and paper. In the past, I'd always avoided people who were connected to anything I regarded as supernatural, mainly because I was frightened they'd tell me something bleak about my future. After what I'd recently been through, this reasoning was now trivial and I couldn't wait to make an appointment with Brian, a psychic who lived in the Perth suburb of Leederville.

The following week, during the twenty-minute drive to Brian's house, I wondered what a psychic would look like. Would he have long hair and a beard, wear long robes and clink a little bell? I could not deny being apprehensive about the meeting, but something urged me on.

I reached the top of the steep driveway just as a tall man with a moustache emerged from the garage swinging a can of paint. I was staggered when he introduced himself as Brian and in that instant my preconceived ideas about psychics went up in smoke. This was just an ordinary man, wearing a very ordinary shirt and trousers; no long hair or beard and no little bell.

The room he ushered me into was furnished with big comfortable lounge chairs and a well-stocked bookcase.

My eyes lit up when they fell upon some of the titles, which I imagined were like the ones I'd been looking for.

I had no idea what to expect from a 'reading', but I sat down and tried to relax. Brian pressed a button on a tape recording machine, then looked across at me and smiled. "We'll tape the session and you can listen to it when you go home."

"Great," I managed.

After settling into his chair he spoke in a gentle tone that immediately put me at ease. We talked for over half an hour about Wayne, his manner of death and my desire to know more on the subject of whether or not people died.

Then Brian said, "Wayne is with you often. He's saying, 'Do you remember when we burnt those potatoes Mum? They were wrapped in foil and we put them in the coals and cooked them too long. They were ruined and we couldn't eat them.'"

Of *course* I remembered! Suddenly I became light-headed. "Ooh. I feel strange. And *look*," I said, putting my arm forward to show Brian that I'd come out in goose bumps.

"That's just confirmation that he's here my dear," he said, and then continued as though I hadn't interrupted, "And I feel I have to talk about peas – fresh green peas, not frozen ones. He's saying he was there when you bought some and when you bought that book, not so long ago."

Brian was right! We were usually happy with frozen peas, but on that shopping day – the very day I found the book by Doris Stokes – fresh peas were cheap and they were extra crisp, so I bought some. How could this man know about those peas? And was it true Wayne was near me often? Did he help me find that book? And was he here now in some kind of ghostly body?

As if seeing my inner dilemma, Brian waved his hand towards the bookshelves and said, "You'll be reading many books like these in the years to come and they'll give you a lot of the answers you're seeking. If you like, afterwards I'll tell you where you can find a shop that specialises in books like these."

I had to calm my enthusiasm. "Oh, yes please. I've looked everywhere…"

Brian nodded his understanding. Then he leaned back, closed his eyes and said, "I have a message for you."

Message? Hey! What kind of message did he mean?

I sat perfectly still, not taking my eyes off him, waiting for something to happen. Several seconds passed in silence before he spoke.

"It may sound harsh to you at this time, but from this experience you will help a considerable number of people in your life ahead. They will come to you for you will have knowledge, and because you have personally suffered, they will be able to relate to you deeply. In about three years' time you will have had a lot more pieces of the jigsaw given to you, whereby you will know inside yourself, you will have a conviction grown within you of the reality and the truth of it all. You will know inside. By the time you are in your fifties, you will have a lot of knowledge and many other experiences will have happened to you, both of the psychic and of the spiritual nature. You will be shown your son quite clearly. Quite, quite clearly. The point about it all is why? For you will be able to help others. You will be able to talk to them about what has happened to you, the depression, the anxiety,

the heartbreak, plus you are going to become a depository of knowledge in this rather sad but specialised field. It has already begun, for you have already done so much more heart seeking than you have ever done in your life. And it will continue, for you will find yourself wanting to know a bit more, and a bit more and you will continue like this to the end of your days. The law of cause and effect is a perpetual law. A cause happens, the effect occurs, which produces another cause. You are in no position to judge your life, or the effect of your life, but you will begin to get an understanding when you are in your early fifties of why it happened and how you have gained from it, and have been able to help others. No one will voluntarily acquire this specialized knowledge or want to get it, but it has occurred and you will know the reality of it all when you see him being shown to you. You will see him for only a few seconds, but you will see so very, very clearly, and it will take you through to the rest of your life, for you will know what you have seen.'

When Brian finished talking, he opened his eyes and sighed. Then he removed the tape from the machine and handed it to me, saying, "That's all I can do for you today my dear. I hope I've been of some help."

I was disappointed that the session had finished, but I was very glad of the tape. Instead of focusing on Brian's words during the delivery of the message, I was so busy wondering where the words were coming from and how this stuff worked that I missed a lot of what he'd said.

Many questions were in my mind but for now were to remain unanswered. There was just one thing I wanted to know before I left. It was my understanding that people like Brian were born with their abilities and if you were behind the door when such things were handed out, you missed out forever. As we walked towards the door I asked, "When did you discover you were psychic, Brian?"

"I began to develop when I was in my late twenties," he said. "And things happened very fast from then on."

"Oh. I see," I said, and turned away so he wouldn't see me roll my eyes. This put a new light on things. What did he mean, 'develop?' Could I trust him now that I knew he wasn't a 'real' psychic – one that hadn't been *born* that way? True, he had given me information that nobody else, especially a stranger, could possibly know, but maybe he was using some mind-reading trick. And for all I knew he might have just made up that so-called message. So I was still uncertain.

As I left his house, Brian directed me to the Theosophical Bookshop in the next suburb and said, "You'll be guided by your own intuition to buy the books you're ready to be reading at this stage of your search. I wish you well."

I went straight to the shop and my heart raced when I saw the row upon row of books with titles that, as far as I had found, were not available in ordinary bookshops. Feeling like a kid in a lolly shop, I examined the different sections.

'Eastern Philosophies?' That didn't strike a chord. 'Psychometry?' Never heard of it. 'Mediumship?' I'd heard the word but wasn't sure what it meant. 'Telepathy?' I knew what that was, but it still didn't sound right for me. 'Zen?' *What?* 'Psychic Development?' I stopped in my tracks. There were books on the subject! After what Brian had just told me, perhaps this was where I was meant to begin reading. I couldn't wait to start and after buying several books in that section hurried off home.

Chapter 4

The first book had a chapter on meditation, with a warning that the reader should be pure of mind and intention. I put the book down and, after thinking about myself, concluded that my intentions must be pretty well pure, because I would never want to hurt anyone. I wasn't too sure about my mind being pure though because I wasn't without a skeleton in my closet. Nevertheless, I thought it wouldn't hurt to put one of the meditations into practice.

I found the place I was looking for in the book. 'Sit with your back straight, or lie down comfortably,' I read.

I made myself comfortable lying on the lounge and then went on reading. Apparently we had things called *chakras* situated throughout the body and the idea was to relax, breathe deeply into each area and concentrate on these chakras that were also called 'energy centres'.

Chakras are energy centres along our spine, existing in our etheric bodies, i.e., not our physical bodies. There are many documented exercises and meditations for concentrating energy on the chakras and these contribute to their strength and growth. I later learnt that we can also contribute to this growth in our daily lives by, for example, practising non-judgement and detachment; not being critical, being generous, showing genuine compassion and forgiveness, loving fellow human beings and animals and most of all, by loving ourselves.

I put the book on the floor, then, nicely relaxed, arms by my sides, I started breathing into each area as instructed. To my horror, after only a couple of minutes, both my arms slowly lifted into the air. I became dizzy and felt what I can only describe as a 'presence,' as though I wasn't just 'me' any more. Next, there were involuntary movements of my tongue and in my mouth and sensations in my throat. It was as if someone was trying to speak – and for sure it wasn't me!

I didn't breathe for what seemed like forever, but I knew there was no help coming and it was up to me to control the situation. I forced myself to sit up, shook my head and stumbled to the kitchen for a drink of water. Gradually the sensations subsided and soon I was normal again.

After Wayne's death I believed nothing could frighten me, but I was scared out of my wits and thought that because my mind wasn't completely pure there was no one to blame but myself.

I tried to put the whole episode aside, but whatever had transpired that day must have created something that couldn't simply be turned off. For instance, while reading my books, whenever I came upon some new information, my head would nod as though in agreement. The same thing happened if I was just sitting in the sun thinking it was a lovely day. Also, it didn't matter where I was or what I was doing, the dizziness would strike and with it came a 'knowing' that I was not alone.

I couldn't think of a way to tell anyone what was happening to me, not even my family, and many times I had to isolate myself from people for a while until I felt all right again. I feverishly searched my books for a simple explanation, but if the right words were there, I couldn't find them.

Matthew and his girlfriend Angela visited one Saturday afternoon about a month after that first alarming experience. I made coffee and we sat down to have a chat. We were looking through some photos when, without warning, I felt dizzy; my eyelids drooped, my body went limp, my tongue moved around in my mouth and I started to sway in the chair. I slurred my words as I asked Matthew to get me some water. He quickly went to the kitchen and filled a glass, but when he held it out to me I couldn't lift my hand to take it, so he put it to my mouth and I drank it down. When he sat down again, he and Angela stared at me in silence.

With great effort, I gathered what strength I could, made it unsteadily to the bathroom and closed the door. What was happening to me? I splashed my face with water and put a wet cloth on my forehead. Soon my head cleared and I went back to the kitchen where Matthew and Angela were still sitting at the table.

"Are you okay, Mum?" Matthew asked. They both looked very concerned.

Matthew was aware of the books I was reading, and had shown he more or less accepted my new interests, but still I couldn't bring myself to open up to him. I tried to appear nonchalant. "Yes, thanks. I don't know what happened there, but I feel much better now."

As they later kissed me goodbye, the look in their eyes told me they were not convinced.

And neither was I.

Over the weeks that followed, the 'problem' persisted, but was now presenting itself in different forms. Often there was a pressure between my eyes, and the top of my scalp buzzed. Several times each day there was a tingling sensation on parts of my face and scalp and I felt as though someone was touching my hair.

It occurred to me that I might be having some kind of breakdown, so I paid my local doctor a visit.

I walked into his office, determined to tell him every detail, but as I looked at him across his huge desk, I lost my nerve and only explained the tingling feelings.

"Where do you have these sensations?" he wanted to know.

"Sometimes here," I said, putting my hand on the side of my head and face. "And sometimes here," I said, touching the top of my head.

He took some notes and then asked, "When do these things happen?"

I thought about it. "Umm…I'm not sure. They just seem to come and go at odd times."

He leaned back in his chair. "Well, do you know how long they last?" I sensed his rising impatience.

I tried to remember, but my mind was all over the place. "No, I'm not sure," I answered weakly.

He leaned further back in his chair. The possibility that he might fall made me smile nervously and a squeaky sound escaped my lips.

His face grew stern and he levelled his chair as he glared at me over the top of his glasses. "Well, Mrs. Templeton," he said shortly. "What you're describing doesn't fit into any of the patterns we know of. I thought at first you might have something called shingles, but the areas you've been showing me are somewhat random and non-specific, would you agree?"

I nodded soberly.

"And you can't tell me how long these sensations last, nor at what times you feel them?"

By this time I was feeling pretty stupid and close to tears. I shook my head, wondering if I should have nodded.

With a superior air, the doctor continued, "So I'm sorry, I can't help you, but I'll give you a prescription for some tranquillizers, because I do think this is a nervous reaction after what you've been through."

As I drove home, frustrated and confused, I thought I must be losing my mind. I felt deserted and isolated and needed someone to save me from… from what? I had no idea.

Chapter 5

I could think of only one person who might be able to help me – my sister Maree who lived in Sydney. I knew she was interested in things of an unusual nature, but wasn't sure what those 'things' were. Did it matter? No. It was her difference I cared about. I knew she once took lessons from our grandmother Hettie Templeton, a numerologist and author. Hettie had been highly sought after as an advisor and teacher and once had her own talk-back program on Radio 2GB in Sydney. When I was about 18 years old, Nanna asked if I'd like to join the class too. But when I looked at one of her books, I closed it very quickly when I came upon a part that read, 'To awaken the higher faculties of the soul…we cannot afford to leave the divine life of God out of anything that we do.' I associated words like 'God' and 'divine' with religion, in which I had no interest. Needless to say I didn't do those lessons. Unfortunately it took years for me to learn that there was wisdom in her words, and that they weren't used in reference to structured religion.

I spent some time thinking about the best way to contact Maree. I couldn't trust myself to phone her because I didn't think I'd be able to verbally express my situation clearly. I decided to write a letter – the hardest letter I've ever written.

Without mentioning my stress or depression, I told her of my interest in the Doris Stokes book and others like it. Then I casually added that unexplainable things were happening to me, and I needed to find out more about psychic development.

As I waited for a reply, I worried what her reaction would be. Would she send in the people with the straitjackets? Would she phone and tell me to pull myself together?

A week later, I was waiting at the letter box when the mailman handed me a thick letter. I gave an excited yelp when I saw it was from Maree, and raced inside, nervously ripping open the envelope as I went. I quickly counted the pages. Seven! Well, they were only small pages, but a thrill of anticipation rippled through my body, then tears of relief began to flow as I started to read. 'I was very pleased to receive such a letter from you at last, and it makes me happy that your search has begun!'

It was unbelievable! Maree knew what I was talking about! And as I continued reading I was overjoyed to find that she seemed not at all shocked by anything in my letter. Clearly we were speaking the same language.

Maree suggested I join a meditation group, or circle as it was called, so I could be with people who had the same interests. 'When you find a group, you'll know whether it's right for you or not,' she said. 'People who go to these groups feel there's more to life than is generally believed. I'm trying to help you in a psychic-development/ spiritual way, and this kind of development doesn't happen overnight; it can take a very long time. Some people dedicate their whole lives to finding answers. And you see, to understand *psychic* experiences, you need to learn about the *spiritual* side of the subject as well.'

There were those religious-sounding words again! Maree wouldn't mislead me, so where did this 'spiritual' part come in? Then I recalled that Brian had said in his message that I would have experiences both of a psychic and spiritual nature. I wondered if I'd opened a can of worms.

From that day, Maree and I telephoned or wrote to each other regularly, and she was always helpful as well as strongly supportive. However, I still needed to deal with the things that were happening to me, so one day I explained the details to her more fully. "If you ask me," she said, "I think you're just developing a gift or two, and they'll soon sort themselves out."

Gifts? What were 'gifts'?

A week or more later, our local paper ran an advertisement for a beginners' meditation group. I guessed this was the kind of group Maree was talking about. The ad read that the first meeting would be at 7.30 that night and the cost was five dollars. This seemed a lot to pay, but since the address was nearby I was eager to go along.

Had I known what was in store for me I would have stayed at home. In bed. With my head under the blankets!

A stooped, thin, middle-aged man with glasses let me into the house, and smiled as he said, "Hello, my name's Roger."

"I'm Amie," I replied. "And I haven't been to one of these groups before."

He showed me into a room where several people were settling themselves into chairs arranged in a circle. "Then you'll be right at home," he said pleasantly. "Neither have any of these other people."

We briefly introduced ourselves, and Roger waited until we were quiet before dimming the lights.

"I'll describe a scene, and you try to stay with me while you follow along with your imagination," he said. "Try not to go to sleep," he added jokingly. "It happens quite often." Then he spoke in a slower, calming voice. "Relax and close your eyes, and imagine you're walking beside a creek on a nice sunny day. You go to the edge of the creek, and you see small fish swimming in the clear water. There are animals, birds and flowers all around you."

After about fifteen minutes of leading us in this manner he said, "Now I want you to bring your mind back into this room, and when you're ready, open your eyes."

So far so good. I had no trouble visualising as he spoke, and was pleased that nothing out of the ordinary had taken place.

After giving us a short break, Roger again asked us to relax and close our eyes, then said, "For this exercise, I'd like you to turn your thoughts inwards, and with your mind, breathe into your body from the top of your head, then breathe out through your feet, deep into the earth."

I did as he instructed, but immediately I was filled with a buzzing kind of energy. If Roger was still talking I didn't hear him. My eyelids felt like lead and I couldn't open them. Then my heart started beating wildly and I began involuntarily taking deep breaths. Foreign words came out of my mouth and didn't stop for about fifteen or twenty seconds. Then an overwhelming sadness entered my body, and tears flooded down my cheeks. From somewhere deep inside came a wailing voice. "My heart! My heart!" Just as with the foreign language, it was my voice, yet it was not I who was speaking.

I heard gasps around me, then Roger's voice filtered through. "It's okay. It's okay."

"I think I'm dying," came the distressed voice of the 'person' within me.

There was a short silence, and then Roger spoke again. This time his voice was shaking. "It's all right. Be calm. Have a look at the body you're in, and you'll see that it isn't yours."

My chin dropped to my chest and my hands turned over backwards and forwards in my lap as though being studied through my closed eyelids. Then my hands came up to my face and my fingers moved over the contours. "This is not me! This is not my body!" the voice cried in alarm.

"No, that's right. And if you think about it, you'll see that you have no pain," urged Roger, his voice still shaking.

As these words were spoken, my body relaxed a little, and the voice came again, calmer this time. "I haven't got any pain."

"That's right," said Roger. Through my fog I thought he sounded relieved. "Now," he went on, "I want you to look for a light. Look for a light, and go towards that light."

"Oh! I can see a light," the voice said in awe. "Oh! And I can see my Mother!"

Instantly the energy changed, then gradually my breathing and heartbeat returned to normal.

When I opened my eyes, Roger was standing in front of me, a shocked look frozen on his face. He spoke sharply, his eyes boring into mine. "What the hell was *that* supposed to be?"

I wanted to ask if he'd like to change places, then *he* could tell *me!* But I was still groggy, and when I opened my mouth, no words came out.

"Learn to control it!" he said harshly. "And buy yourself a cross! It will protect you, but you're *never* to take it off!" He paused a moment. "You're lucky I know how to deal with lost souls! And do you realize you've set these people back..." he waved his arm around the room at the group as he searched for words, "who knows how far!"

I couldn't look at anyone, but their silence told me they were stunned by what they'd witnessed. Totally humiliated, I found my way to the front door and out into the street.

Back home, still intensely disturbed, I tried to understand what was wrong with me. Was I possessed? I'd read that if you weren't careful you could attract negative energies that stayed with you for years, wreaking havoc along the way. But I'd also read that a possessed person could be induced to do things they would not normally do in their daily lives, and I didn't think this was happening in my case.

I didn't want to buy a cross because I thought that to do so would be the final step to admitting I had some permanent, sinister problem. I also believed crosses were only for religious people, and I just 'knew' I wouldn't find my answers in that direction.

My experience with Roger became a constant reminder that I was impaired in some way. As a result, I felt dirty and degraded for a long time, until I eventually realized that his treatment of me was shameful, and he lacked the responsibility required for someone in charge of a meditation group. I now believe that he was hiding behind his own fears and lack of knowledge about the situation that confronted him.

In desperation, the day after that terrible humiliation, I phoned a church where I heard they did something called 'speaking in tongues'.[2]

The Pastor listened as I explained what had happened at Roger's house. I mentioned only that I'd begun to speak a foreign language, thinking I'd be overdoing it if I mentioned the person with the heart condition.

"Were you praying at the time?" he asked. "No, I was at a meditation group."

"Oh *Dear!*" He sounded horrified. "There are lots of entities out there just *waiting* for people like you, and you'll need to read your Bible *every* day for a *very* long time before you free yourself of this influence."

I felt sick, but he hadn't finished.

"Don't you know not to dabble in such activities? You need to keep your mind on God so that such things don't happen to you. Have you thought of having an exorcism?"

My mind was racing. This couldn't be happening. I mumbled something and hung up.

I wondered if this was as low as a person might go before they contemplated suicide. Numb and emotionless, I believed I had no alternative but to buy a cross. I went straight to a jewellery store and chose a small gold one with a tiny ruby in the centre, putting it on as I left the

---

[2] References to 'speaking in tongues' can be found in the Bible. Controversy surrounded the subject then as it does now. For examples, see 1 Cor. 12:10, 12:30-31, 14:1-40. Also, the Internet has information on the subject

shop. Would it help to protect me in some way from the frightening things that were happening to me? I didn't know.

I stayed close to home and kept my head in my books, but as the weeks passed, I found no words that explained 'me.' Still, there was no stopping me now that I'd come this far. It was not a question of whether or not to continue, for as I saw it I had no choice. It was impossible to get on with life in my present fragile situation, and it was also obvious that to continue my search I needed more outside help.

Chapter 6

The memory of the disastrous incident at Roger's house still made me shudder, but even so, when an advertisement for another group appeared in the local paper I gave it some serious thought. 'Development Group for Beginners' the ad read. Dare I go? Would I again be stepping from the frying pan into the fire? From what I could work out, this type of group was my only means of meeting people who might sooner or later be able to help me. Maybe in amongst there somewhere was the answer to the mess I was in, so I made up my mind to give it a try.

The group was held on Wednesday nights at 7.30 in the suburb of Bayswater, about a ten-minute drive from home. It was run by two ladies named Sue and Val at Val's house and they asked only a dollar to cover the cost of a light supper. The nine other men and women who attended were beginners like me and ranged in age from about thirty to seventy.

During these meetings, Sue and Val talked to us on a variety of interesting subjects like chakras, guides and the Ascended Masters. In these discussions they often used words and phrases I'd never heard before, but something in their sound caused the familiar surges of energy to fill my body and I had to continually fight against losing control. Whenever the surges reached dangerous levels, I took time out in the toilet until I returned to normal. I spent lots of time in the toilet! However, my efforts to fight the surges meant that during most of those talks my mind was elsewhere. I was keen to show interest in what I was being taught, but it wasn't easy.

It was after the third week that Sue asked, "Has anyone noticed anything different about themselves since coming to the group?"

I sat quietly, not saying a word. I didn't want to attract attention to myself like the time at Roger's place.

One lady, Rhonda, said, "Someone or something keeps touching my hair very lightly."

My antennae went up.

Then an older man, Robert added, "Yes, I feel that too and sometimes my scalp and face feel odd as well."

"It's spirit contact," Sue explained. "You've shown interest in finding out about yourselves and your spiritual awareness is growing. Our psychic abilities are awakened as our soul slowly unfolds."

I couldn't contain my excitement. "I know what you mean!" I tried not to shout. "That happens to me!"

"It means someone's close to you," Val added. "The thing is that you always need to check who's there, because sometimes they like to play games with you."

I was swept along by my own enthusiasm. "Well, what do I do when they want to speak through me?" I asked. "There nearly always seems to be someone there ready to talk."

The other group members were looking at me. The last thing I'd wanted to do was attract attention to myself again. I wished I'd kept my mouth shut!

Sue said, "It sounds as though you just need to learn to keep it in control."

"But I didn't know what the touches were until now and I don't know *how* to control the other bit." I answered sullenly.

Val explained, "Always ask with your mind if they're from the Light – from God. If they are, they'll let you know. Ask three times, if you feel the need. If they don't answer you, then demand that they leave and don't give them any more of your attention. And if you think it's a lost soul, tell them to go to the Light."

It sounded right, but I also thought it sounded too easy. I was horribly affected by what was happening to me – not just the touches on the hair or face that others were experiencing – yet Sue and Val were treating it as an everyday event. When they offered no further advice, I could only surmise that they thought I understood more than I was saying, when in truth I felt unworthy for foolishly bringing this problem upon myself and thought I was losing my sanity.

In any case, away from the group, whenever the energy swept through my body, which could be several times a day, I did my best to stay in control. I was very distressed – imagining they were all lost souls – and forgot about asking if they were from the Light. I'd no sooner send one away, when another surge, or presence, would replace it. Or maybe it was the same one. I had no way of knowing. Sometimes these bombardments lasted an hour or more and I was left limp with exhaustion. I felt helpless, yet too conscious of my tenuous situation to seek more advice from Val and Sue. However I kept going to the group because for one thing, strangely, I'd begun to feel comfortable there, but also I knew of nowhere else to go.

We were introduced one night to something called 'inspirational writing' – which, I understood, was a form of channelling using this simple technique:

Relax.

Visualise yourself surrounded with white light for protection.

Say a prayer requesting that you be attuned to the highest guidance available to you at this time, then relax, and then listen.

Always keep in mind that lower entities cannot teach you anything, so if you doubt your connection it's wise to begin again.

Invite your guides to talk with you.

Watch your thoughts, and when you detect words that you believe you are not thinking, write them down.

Even if you find only one such word in your head – write it down. If you don't, you might not receive anything further because your guides will think you didn't 'get' that first word.

I sat with my pen poised above the paper, but at first the thoughts that filled my head were those of inadequacy. Once I was able to clear my mind I could feel a pressure between my eyes (at the 'third eye' chakra centre) and in the centre of the top of my head (at the 'crown chakra') and there was a feeling in my left ear as if some small insect had flown into it. As I turned my concentration to the exercise, words came to me right away and I wrote the following:

We ask that you consider for a moment the ways of the world. There are signs to look for when dealing with humanity.

1. *Is in Love*

2. *Hope*

3. *Freedom*

4. *Peace*

5. *Beauty*

6. *Understanding*

7. *Kindness*

8. *Fulfilment of duty to God.*

You have written what we have asked of you. Our communication will improve as you gain deeper understanding. We are here to help and guide you, since this is your wish.

I asked in my head if there was further communication for me and the answer came as quick as a flash:

Yes. There is much more that we would impart. This cannot be today, however. We will be near you when you need us. The ways of the world are becoming clearer to you and you will advance with this knowledge. Since you have made it your wish that we help you, you can now move forward in your search. It is not an easy path, and although the heights that can be attained are within your reach, it is you alone who can tread the way. We will go now until next time.

I put my pen down and stared at the page. 'Wow! Where did *that* come from?' I wondered aloud. I didn't understand it all, but apart from number 8, 'Fulfilment of duty to God,' I thought it was wonderful and couldn't wait to show Sue and Val.

I was disillusioned when, after reading it, they gave each other a knowing smile. "That's good Amie," said Sue, "Just keep practising at home."

Deflated, I looked again at my sheet of paper and wondered what secret they were sharing. Okay, so it wasn't such a great piece of writing, but I thought it wasn't too bad for my first attempt. Maybe they were amused because I said I didn't like that bit about God being thrown in there. 'Oh well,' I thought, 'they'll learn.'

I soon found it was I who would do the learning, when the subject of God came up again a week or two later. I couldn't see why it was being discussed at a meditation group, because I thought such groups were distinctly separate from religion.

I tried not to listen and looked everywhere but at Sue while she talked. There was no way I was going to be drawn into this discussion. But her words still drifted through to me and when I heard her say that God was in everything — in the trees, the clouds and even in us – something made me take interest. By the end of the evening, I'd perceived that an intangible link existed between meditation, spiritual development and religion. Words like 'God', 'spiritual' or 'divine,' seemed to be interchangeable, meaning that such expressions could be used even when a person *wasn't* talking about religion. This was thought-provoking, but it was also a lot to take in, so it all went into my 'too-hard basket' – for the time being.

One morning, only days later, I awoke knowing a change had taken place within me. I was no longer as fearful as when I'd bought my cross. Roger had told me never to take it off, implying that dire consequences would follow if I did so. In fear, I'd complied with his warning, but it was only now that I wondered how I could have given a piece of jewellery such power over me. I got out of bed and, in a daring act of defiance, took the cross from around my neck. I stood very still…and waited. Nothing happened. I wasn't struck by lightning. I wasn't attacked by a thousand and one entities. Instead, serenity filled and surrounded me and I knew without doubt that I had taken a step forward. I held the cross and chain in the palm of my hand and looked at it lovingly, then put it away in my jewellery case on the dressing table. After that day, I wore it only when I chose to do so.

Chapter 7

At our group one night, Val said, "I've got a message for you Amie, from someone called Andrea."

I pulled a face. "The only Andrea I know is still alive," I said. "And I don't like her much." Andrea was a neighbour and had been a troublemaker – a real gossip – ever since I'd known her.

"Sometimes the higher self, or soul, of a person can make psychic contact while they're still alive," said Val, "And I'm being asked that you send her love."

"What?" I shrieked. "Send her love! You've got to be joking! No way! She's caused too much trouble in my life with her venomous tongue!"

Val's reply was almost inaudible. "Okay."

I missed the significance of what she was trying to teach me and I cringe now when I think of how little I knew. But, at that moment, I was just relieved she didn't mention the subject again.

The following week we were given some homework and I wasn't aware at the time that the exercise was connected to my being asked to send love to Andrea. It was probably even initiated by my angry response to Val.

"Look in your mirror every morning and say 'I love you,'" Sue said. "Tell yourself that you're beautiful."

Val added, "It's essential that you learn to love everyone, but the place to start is with yourself."

I couldn't imagine anything more distasteful, although I didn't want to appear disagreeable again, so I smiled as though I would do as they asked – but I had no intention of doing so.[3]

A medium called Marge visited the group one evening and after giving messages to two or three people, she addressed a young man, Peter, who sat next to me in the front row. "My, you have an acute sense of smell! Those soap aisles are bothersome to you, aren't they?" she asked.

I turned to look at Peter, waiting for his answer, because recent surgery to the inside of my nose had resulted in an extremely acute sense of smell, forcing me to avoid the washing soap aisles in the supermarket. I thought it would be quite a coincidence if Peter suffered the same unusual ailment.

"Ahh, well, I guess so," he replied.

Marge went on, "And I see you've just bought a new car, or you're thinking about it."

By now I was really puzzled. John and I had just bought a new car! What was going on? Were these messages meant for me? Again I looked at Peter.

"We're thinking about changing our car, yes, but it's not a priority right at the moment," he said.

By this time, I was on the edge of my chair waiting to be noticed. Surely Marge would soon realize her aim was off.

---

[3] When we look in the mirror and tell ourselves that we're beautiful, or simply say 'I love you,' – or even 'Hello, I know you're in there' if you like – we're not talking to our physical self, but to the true beauty of the inner self. Once we begin searching for this real self, life starts to give up her mysteries.

I wanted to wave, but thought that mightn't go down too well, so I gave a little cough, trying to catch her attention. It didn't work.

"You've been thinking of doing an oil painting," Marge was saying to Peter, "But you've been putting it off. Try it. It will be therapeutic for you."

That was the last straw! A friend had recently taken me to an art supplies shop and helped me select paints, brushes, canvases and other materials. 'Oil painting will be therapeutic for you', she'd said! I opened my mouth to speak, but Marge turned away quickly to give another reading to someone at the back of the room.

I leaned closer to Peter and whispered, "Are you thinking of painting?"

Frowning, he shook his head and mouthed, "No."

Yes, sure, I was a beginner and had no idea how mediums came by their information, but there was no logic in what I had just witnessed.

When Marge finished her readings, I hurried to find Sue. "Do you think, um, I mean," I faltered, "Is it possible for someone like Marge to give a message to the wrong person?"

Right away I regretted asking the question.

"No, of course not!" Sue answered tersely. "Marge is an excellent medium and that just couldn't happen."

"Sorry," I said, embarrassed.

Just the same, I believed I was right and that Marge somehow had her wires crossed.[4]

This episode brought about other, more obscure thoughts. It was as though I 'knew' something and with this nebulous knowing came another small measure of self-confidence – like when I took that cross from around my neck – so I made up my mind to stay away from the group for a while to sort out my feelings.

---

[4] As the years passed I discovered that it is certainly possible for mediums to unintentionally deliver a message to the wrong person.

Chapter 8

During the time I was away from the group, my spare time was spent either reading books or practising inspirational writing. The copious flow of information I received from the writing was always encouraging and I longed to share my results with someone. I tried telling a few family friends and acquaintances about my new-found communications, but they usually changed the subject. I could talk to Maree sometimes, but distance was a problem. Matthew and I had discussions now and then about Wayne and on the theory of life after death, but mostly I felt so very lonely.

One day I picked up my pen and wrote to my guides, 'Are you here with me now? I have some questions for you.' I wanted to ask why the pathway was so difficult, and why people turned away when I tried to talk to them.

The response was instantaneous, and I quickly wrote the words that danced in my head.

Seeking knowledge always has its pitfalls. Sometimes hardships are placed in your path as hurdles – to be climbed, not walked around. Even though we are helping you, the path is still uphill. The light is bright enough to blind you. Show caution. Absorb only a little at a time. Tread lightly so as not to offend others, and care not that your words are not always heard. Once the path to self-discovery has been found, there seems no turning back. The path seems long and rocky as it steadily ascends. The higher it ascends, the broader the view. The broader the view, the least inclined is the individual to abandon the trek. The path is narrow. Aim for the heights and be assured of keeping to the path – the true path. Love abounds. Helpers await your needs.

Seek and you will find. What it is you are seeking can only be revealed as knowledge and understanding unfold within you. This life has been given to experience tribulations unlike any you have known. Coping, keeping control of the mind, bringing knowledge to others and helping to ease their pain. These are the reasons. Do not question them. Let the love flow from your heart. Material things, as you have learnt, are of no importance. Try not to pity those who do not yet wish to join you, rather pray from them, that they will soon come to understand in their own time, and in their own way. Your pity will be wasted. The time could be better spent in learning, meditating, and spreading love.

Heartache has settled like a cloud over many souls. Still many more feel they are unable to cross the bridge unaided. Reach out your hand to them. If they should take it, then you will have done what is best for them. If they choose to ignore it, then leave them be. You cannot return for them, for learning makes this impossible – as your inner heart will tell you.

We will keep them afloat until they learn to swim – as you are swimming – and until they see that they have been floundering in a sea of nothingness. God bless you.

As well as answering my unasked questions, these words comforted me, and I felt I'd found a dear friend.

Only days after that communication, something different came through.

We wish to teach you the language of the upper world.

As I wrote those words, I frowned. Upper world? It sounded like something from a fairy tale. Despite my doubts, I telepathically replied, "I would love to learn this language. Can I have a word to begin?"

Immediately my head became full of words. It was like looking at many banners continuously changing place; like little children fighting to be first in line.

Battling to keep focused, I plucked out one of the words, and as I wrote it down I asked, "Is that spelt 'Senga?'"

That is how it sounds, which will suffice for now.

I wrote as fast as I could, but knew I was missing lots of words along the way.

Huska Peanu

Seek avasti Samsenka

Harvoo-aki Kuanti

Then there was a pause, the words faded away, and my 'communicator' said, *'Amie, these will be enough words for now.'*

I was in awe of what was taking place, and didn't want the session to end, but all I could think to ask was, "Is this really coming from you?"

'Yes, those and other words that appeared too much for you at this time.'

'Yes, my mind was flowing with them. They were all very strange.'

'Strangeness is only that the tongue is un-used to them. I will go now.'

I was fascinated with this communication but still had my doubts about it being from a reliable source, so when I saw Matthew later in the week I thought I'd get his opinion.

"What do you think of this?" I asked, showing him my notes.

When he'd finished reading he asked, "Where did you get this, Mum?"

What would he think? I watched his face. "In my head," I said.

He raised his eyebrows.

I considered my words carefully. "Well," I said haltingly, "It just sort of came to me like thoughts, and I wrote it down."

He rubbed his chin. "Hmm. Do you know what it means?"

I shook my head and laughed. "No. I've got no idea."

"I'll tell you what," he said. "I'll go to the library and check it out."

"What a great idea," I said enthusiastically.

Matthew came back a few hours later and we looked over his notes. He'd found two words that were close to 'senga'. The first was 'singha', defined as being from Sanskrit.[5] The second word was 'sankhya', also from Sanskrit, meaning 'one of the six orthodox schools of Hindu Philosophy teaching an eternal interaction of Spirit and Matter.'

The only other word close to mine was 'avesta' instead of 'avasti', which, the reference book had stated, was from Zoroastrianism. We checked my dictionary, and found this description of Zoroaster: 'Persian believed to have lived

---

[5] An ancient language of India dating from the first millennium BC.

in the 6th Century BC, founder of the dualistic religious system of the Magi and ancient Persia that survives among the Parsees. Its scriptures, the Zend-Avesta, teach that the lord of goodness and light and creator of mankind is ceaselessly at war with the evil spirits of darkness.'

I didn't know enough to take in these ancient and meaningful origins. I only noticed that the words weren't exactly the same as those I'd received, so my enthusiasm faded somewhat.

Matthew seemed interested yet disappointed, and as he left he said, "Oh well, it was a fascinating exercise." We didn't speak of it to each other again.

The word *computer* wasn't even in my vocabulary back then, and when I couldn't find any reference to a 'language of the upper world' in my dictionaries, I thought the whole thing must have come from my imagination.

For some years after that day, I only tuned in to the messages on rare occasions, for while the source itself seemed limitless, I'd lost trust in what I was receiving. I thought I'd been deceived by entities playing tricks, and that the communications were from the same source as the lost souls and the foreign language that I spoke, which in my mind was negative. I know now that my fear of being deluded prevented me from seeing another truth that was knocking on my door.

Sixteen years later, while researching the Kabbalah (also spelt Kabbala, Cabbala or Qabala) on the internet, I nearly fell off my chair in shock when I came upon numerous references to 'the language of the Upper World.' I had neither seen nor heard those words from the day I received them until that very moment. I believe that because my own channels were not clear, the reception was vague. Also, because language is a limited form of expression it can be difficult to decipher a complex telepathic communication.

Chapter 9

We are an eternal soul wearing a physical body.

As I read those words I knew them to be true, and a piece of the jigsaw fell into place.

I rested the book on my lap and gazed out through our lounge room window. A lady was walking along the street and I wondered if she knew she was a soul wearing a physical body. Did she know she was an eternal 'energy being' wearing her body like an overcoat? I'd always believed we had a soul, but previously imagined we were a superb physical body with an indefinable soul lurking somewhere inside. But now I knew I had it back to front and that the physical body exists for the purpose of the soul to express itself not only in this lifetime, but also, as I was later to learn, in many other lifetimes.

I was alone in the house. Quiet music played on the radio and thoughts from years gone by came drifting through my mind.

I was eight or nine and ready for bed one night when, for no reason that I can remember, I stood in front of the dressing- table mirror and looked into my eyes. "That's only where your *eyes* are," I said aloud to myself. "That's not where 'you' are. If your eyes were in your shoulder, or in your leg or your back, you'd still think *you* were behind them looking out. Just because they're in your head makes you think *you* are *only* in your head. But you're not. You can be anywhere, all over the place in your body; and even if you were blind, you'd still be in there somewhere."

Startled by my own thoughts I dived into bed, first making sure the door was open so I wouldn't be in the dark.

Later that night I awoke to see a 'golden man' sitting near the end of the bed at my feet. He was glowing so brightly I couldn't see his features, but I knew he was facing me. Afraid to move, I called out for mum, but before she came the man dissolved before my eyes. Mum just smiled and said, "You've had a bad dream," and went back to bed.

Around the same time I was walking to my friend Dianne's house one afternoon, when it struck me that for the last several steps my feet had not touched the footpath – I was walking above it. With this realisation, I instantly found myself again at ground level. I turned nervously and looked at the section of path I'd somehow passed across, but saw nothing out of the ordinary. I looked around hoping to find a witness but the street was empty.

I ran the rest of the way to Dianne's place. "You'll never guess what!" I said breathlessly. "I walked off the ground on my way here. I don't know how it happened."

Dianne laughed. "Don't be silly," she said. "You can't walk *off* the ground. You walk *on* it!"

After that, I thought I'd better not talk to anyone else about it.

Street lights and bare light bulbs intrigued me because I saw what I called 'rainbows' around each one. I thought everyone could see these colours, but when I mentioned it to a school teacher one day, she smirked and said, "What a stupid thing to say!"

In my early teens my younger sister Sonya and I frequently took long walks. We talked about the universe and tried to work out how it began. If it was night, we looked at the stars and wondered how they got there and whether there were other people up there somewhere. And how did the stars just sit there? Where did they begin and end?

On one such walk I stopped and turned to Sonya. "Sometimes I feel like I could just peel my skin off and be free!" I said. "You know, just step out of my shell as if this body was only some kind of protection."

Sonya didn't comment, but her eyes were wide as she gave me a sideways glance.

"I've always believed I could fly," I explained, "But I could never work out how to do it in my normal body. Perhaps if I peeled off my skin I could do it."

Not so many years ago, I was out walking one hot summer evening and when I was half a kilometre or so from home I saw a man get off a bus at a corner about fifty metres away. He wore a suit and carried a briefcase and as he began walking in my direction I saw that he seemed to lack energy in his step. I imagined that he set off early every morning to catch his bus and now he was arriving home after dark obviously tired, having spent all day at his place of work.

I watched as he turned into the driveway of one of the new houses that lined each side of the road. Spotlights blazed in the backyard and children were splashing about and laughing in the swimming pool.

I stood in front of that house for a minute or two, wondering what was wrong with the picture I was looking at. Then, as

I analysed my thoughts, it was clear there must be more to life than what that family was experiencing. This man left early in the morning five days a week, went to his job and returned after dark, not seeing his family or his new house all day. This same scene was being repeated millions of times throughout the world. Houses – little boxes – sitting side by side; people running back and forth to work like ants in a frenzy; each family having its own financial and emotional problems. Then everyone gets old and dies! *If* they live that long.

Yes, there definitely had to be more to life than what, by all accounts, the vast majority of people on earth were doing every day.

Then the penny dropped as I realised that my own family was in there somewhere too. I was thirty-three, worked full time and had three boys aged fourteen, twelve and ten. My husband John was a long-distance truck driver and away for days at a time. We were doing well financially and had just built our first home in the suburbs of Perth. But I could now see that time was passing us by; we would soon get old and be gone from this earth – but for what reason?

I'd heard somewhere that we were here to learn, but that didn't make much sense to me. I remember telling a work colleague Janice once that as far as I was concerned it wasn't much good being an Einstein or having any goals in life, because when we died our knowledge and dreams would all die with us – so we might just as well sit in a corner and wait for the end to come. Looking back, I wondered what Janice must have thought about me and my views at the time.

Returning to the present, I picked up my book but couldn't concentrate on reading. My mind was trying to relate those earlier thoughts and experiences to what I was now learning. It was becoming clear that these various pieces were all part of another side of me – a side not understood by most people I knew.

Just then I caught a movement out of the corner of my eye and turned my head to see the venetian blind cord swinging back and forth. I sat motionless as I searched the room, moving only my eyes, but saw nothing unusual. Our German shepherd, Rex, was nowhere to be seen, so he couldn't have bumped the cord.

Then, a loud click and the music on the radio stopped. I got up and walked over to the machine. The power switch on the wall was in the OFF position. I let out a cry. Rex bounded in from the yard and stood beside me barking crazily and as I reached out to reassure him bright red flashes burst from his throat in every direction.

I jerked my hand back and yelled, "Shit!"

I stared at Rex, fearful of what might happen next, but, quiet now, he just trotted outside again.

I threw myself on the lounge and curled up with my knees under my chin. I felt exposed, defenceless and angry and wanted to become invisible, vanish, so I wouldn't have to deal with any more of this baloney. One minute I was learning uplifting things and was full of bliss, and the next I was being frightened half to death. "What's going on?" I whimpered aloud to the empty house. "Will someone *please* help me?"

Days turned into weeks. I hardly went out or spoke to anyone, although sometimes, when John was home from a trip, we went to a barbeque or the social club. The sympathetic expressions in the eyes of friends and associates at these gatherings made it clear that while we were both under scrutiny, I was their main focus and I felt patronised. I could never be sure whether the looks were because of Wayne's death, or because of the 'things' they'd probably heard I was 'into' – or both. I wanted to lash out and cry 'STOP! I don't need your pity! I don't need you to tell me whether I'm sane or not!' On the inside my defence mechanism was in full swing, but I was trapped inside my head and felt powerless to give my feelings any outward expression.

And so I preferred to keep to myself and went on reading my books. One I found extremely interesting was Dawn Hill's *Reaching for the Other Side*. While her story differed from mine in detail, it did portray the author's personal struggle on the spiritual path and this comforted me. Her address was included for readers to make contact if they wished, so I sent her a long detailed letter, asking if she could help me with explanations or advice.

As I waited for a reply my stomach nerves jumped every time the mailman came. I became paranoid in the weeks that followed, seldom leaving the house and standing constant guard over the mailbox. I didn't want anyone to see Dawn's letter when it came. I fantasised that it would stand out because it was sure to be a thick letter and her return address would be on the back. The family would ask questions if they saw it and I believed that if they knew what I was doing they'd send me for psychiatric treatment.

One morning about three weeks later I watched from the verandah as a long thick envelope was delivered by the mailman. As soon as he was out of sight, I ran to the letterbox and reached into its darkness. I was full of anticipation and my imagination went berserk. I could see myself reading Dawn's words and finding the answers I was seeking so urgently.

My hand wrapped around the envelope, but when I pulled it out my heart sank. It was my own letter returned to me! The post office stamp across its front read 'No longer at this address.'

Like a robot I stood at the rubbish bin and carefully tore the envelope and its contents to shreds. I was devastated and wondered if I'd ever find my way out of the darkness that surrounded me.

Chapter 10

I was feeling lethargic as I idly browsed through my books the next night and pulled out one called *You Forever* by Tuesday Lobsang Rampa. It was one of the first I'd bought, but because it mentioned molecules, protons, neutrons and atoms and contained scientific-looking drawings, I guessed it was beyond me and had put it back on the shelf.

Now as I leafed through *You Forever,* stopping to read parts that caught my eye, I was mystified because I could easily comprehend phrases that I'd once thought too technical. This change in my level of understanding, I reasoned, must have been due to the spiritual growth that was taking place within me.

Among other metaphysical subjects, Rampa mentioned seeing our own aura in a mirror and said the lighting in the room needed to be dim so we could see the delicate colours more easily. My mind went to the colours around those streetlights and light bulbs. Could this be the same thing?

I later learnt that the aura is an energy field that surrounds all matter. Anything that has an atomic structure has an aura – an energy field. In the human aura, the colours signify our spiritual, emotional and mental condition at the time. It can be weakened by such things as drugs, tobacco, excessive alcohol and negative psychic activity, but its strength can be regained with lots of fresh air and exercise, a balanced diet and good habits. Normally, we need to work on these aspects of ourselves to raise our energy closer to the vibratory rate of the aura, otherwise it's too fast for us to see.

Daylight was fading as I washed my hands in the bathroom the following day and I realized the setting was perfect for an aura-seeing experiment.

The bathroom was rather small and rectangular – bath with shower curtain on the right, washbasin at the end and large mirror on the left.

I relaxed and, as the book suggested, looked in the mirror to the right of my face and allowed my gaze to go out of focus as though looking at something on the other side of the wall.

I was not prepared for what happened next.

Within seconds, the mirror clouded, my image shimmered, then disappeared! I recoiled and staggered backwards. The edge of the bath caught my legs knocking me off balance. I grabbed for the shower curtain, but it ripped from the rail and I fell backwards, landing heavily.

After untangling myself from the curtain, I stood up in the bath and checked the damage. Two bruised elbows, a bump on the head and a sore rear-end for me. Only two curtain rings were in one piece, but thankfully the rail wasn't broken.

I kept one eye on the mirror as I stepped carefully out of the bath. 'It's only a mirror,' I told myself. 'There can't be anything in there to hurt me.'

A part of me scoffed "Oh yeah?"

I pushed those thoughts aside and struggled to assure myself that I wasn't in peril. Then I stood in front of the mirror again. Using my peripheral vision and gazing in the same way as before, I watched, awe-struck, as almost at once the mirror went hazy again. This time my reflection stayed put, but slight changes were occurring that I couldn't clearly distinguish.

Several times I moved my eyes to look directly at my face trying to catch sight of these movements, but with the change of focus my own face returned and I had to begin all over again.

Several tries later, still with no success, I tried a different approach. I shifted my gaze to the tip of my nose. The results were dramatic. My nose changed and my eyes were blue instead of hazel! Everything was different – my skin, the shape of my face, even my hairstyle.

'My God!' I thought. 'None of that is me!'

The vision shimmered and a different face drifted in to replace the first. And after that, another face, replacing the second. Then, as if by way of a grand finale, the mirror dazzled with a pale blue brilliance. In the centre was a pale- blue lady, who looked at me from the mirror until my eyes grew tired and I relaxed my focus.

I swallowed hard. "Holy smoke, what next?" I muttered. Surprisingly, I realized I wasn't frightened, just dumbfounded that such a thing could happen. What did it mean? Where did the faces come from? Why was I able to see them?

I wondered if the same thing would happen each time I looked into the mirror, so for the next week I repeated the exercise every day. Now and again, when I least expected it, I saw fleeting colours of my aura, but otherwise the results were mostly the same – first the faces, not always the same ones – then the 'blue lady'. Once I saw what looked like an American Indian whose lined and leathered skin told me he was very old. I focused on his mouth, but then I saw his lips move as though he was about to speak to me, so I quickly closed my eyes and turned away from the mirror. I didn't mind looking at these faces, but I wasn't ready for conversations with them!

Gradually I came to accept this phenomenon, though I hadn't heard about it before or read anything on the subject. Just the same, it had become a normal part of me and I used the exercise regularly as a point of focus and relaxation.

It wasn't until eighteen years after Wayne's death that I came across a section in *Love Never Dies,* where the author, Margaret Dent, a medium and healer (deceased in February, 2005) was trying to block out the thoughts of other people and began practising self-hypnosis in front of her mirror. However, as soon as she reached a relaxed state she could see different faces in the mirror. She said it scared her in the beginning and she didn't understand until years later that she was becoming 'intuned' – that she was one of those people who could reach that state without any conscious tuning. She also learnt that the other faces were those of her teachers and guides.

Almost two months had passed since my last visit to the development group at Val's house and I thought it was time to go back. It was great to be welcomed by the group which included a new lady – Jan – and I was filled with a renewed confidence.

I wasn't concerned now with what others in the group thought and openly shared my latest experiences with the mirror, my feeling of regular 'presences' and the foreign language episodes that were still occurring. The answers from Sue and Val were the same as before. 'Your psychic abilities are awakening.' 'Your soul is unfolding.' And again they stressed the need for control. But their words didn't 'do it' for me. I still felt something was wrong and needed whatever it was to be fixed. I needed detailed explanations – clear-cut answers – and I needed them *now!* If the presences and language were considered normal, why wasn't anyone else going through the same thing? And why wasn't there anything about 'me' in the books I'd read? From these books I had at least learnt that after a traumatic experience many people went on what was called an 'inner search,' or 'spiritual search', but there were no written instructions on how to put together the bucket of nuts and bolts that had landed on me. (See Note re Kryon at the end of this Chapter)

I was reminded of a story about a man with a deformed leg who hobbled up the mountain to see his guru. Exhausted, he finally arrived and asked the guru what to do about his bad leg. The guru looked at him steadily for a long moment and then said, *'Limp!'*

I could see I needed to do a lot of 'limping'!

As I walked to my car from Val's house that night, I heard Jan, the new group member, call my name. "Have you got a minute?" she asked. "I'd like to talk to you about something."

I wondered what she would want to talk to me about. "Yes, sure," I said. It was a cold night. "Let's sit in my car," I offered.

When we were settled, she said, "After listening to you talk about what's been happening to you, I wondered if you'd like some help."

"I sure would!" I said eagerly.

"I've had similar experiences, that's why I'm in a group, still working on myself," she said.

Experiences similar to *mine*? Wasn't I the only person like me in the world?

"I can't help you get rid of the foreign language unfortunately," she continued. "I think you'll find that's there to stay. But I can help you control it and I'm sure I can help with the other things." Then she asked, "What have you tried already?"

I gave her the details of what Val advised me to do, then said, "And they go for a while, but they just keep coming back! I don't know what I'm doing wrong. What am I supposed to do with them?"

"I'll work with you if you like, but it takes time," she said. "Things change as we learn and grow. If it's been a few months since you worked on yourself, you might find it easier now."

I sighed. "I hope so."

Jan smiled knowingly. "It's okay, you know. You're not going mad. Even that language you're talking about belongs in there somewhere."

I worked with Jan at her house every two or three days for the next four weeks and with perseverance I knew I was making headway. I was doing the same as before, but I'd only tried the procedure on my own. Now, with Jan's help and reassurance, each time I felt a presence of any kind I sent it to the light by using my mind to communicate. I still didn't feel normal though because I could feel something was still there – somewhere. However, the situation had reversed itself to some extent, for 'they' no longer had complete control of me; rather it was *I* who had a degree of control over *them*.

This meant I wasn't 'fixed.' I'd only received a band-aid measure to help me on my way. I treasured what Jan had done for me, although it was unfortunate that she wasn't able to explain the foreign presence. I wondered if I would ever find someone who knew, *really* knew what was the matter with me.

Months went by and at the group I learnt what was meant by Mediumship. With practice, I could relay short messages to members from a deceased relative or friend. I also discovered the meaning of Psychometry[6] – receiving vibrations from jewellery or other items, even people. These vibrations came to me either as feelings, words or

---

[6] Everything from a stone to a human being retains the vibrations of whatever contact they've made during their existence and we can learn to tune in to these vibrations through Psychometry. It is helpful to remember that the more relaxed we are, the more sensitive we become to the serenity of the energies around us.

still pictures, and sometimes it was like watching a movie in my head.

One night we were practising Psychometry and I was holding a bracelet belonging to Myrna, an English lady. In my mind I could see her walking along the hallway of what I imagined was her home. She stopped in front of a long mirror and twirled around, her dress swishing. I was describing this picture to her when I received the word 'swanking.' "Swanking," I said aloud. "I've never heard of that word." Then, addressing everyone present I asked, "What does 'swanking' mean?" But before anyone could answer I said to Myrna, "I'm being told you were swanking."

I heard a stifled giggle or two, then a hush fell over the room. What had I said?

I'd finished the reading anyway and as I walked back towards my seat, another English lady, Mavis, yanked me to one side and hissed, "Swanking means 'showing off' and I think you've just embarrassed Myrna."

I looked across at Myrna. She was glowering at me. I knew she was prim and proper, but I would never knowingly say anything to humiliate her.

I groaned. I guess she thought I was rubbing it in, saying the word 'swanking' not once but *three* times! I could do nothing but apologise.

Afterwards I lectured myself about being more careful in future. It was clear I still had a lot to learn.

* * *

Kryon, in *A New Dispensation,* channelled by Lee Carroll, has these words of wisdom when referring to the new energies that are emerging in these later years:

> Think of this metaphor: You are a carpenter. You go to sleep one night and wake up to find that your old tools are still there, but next to them is a case that says, *There are new power tools in this case...* Some won't want the new tools. Some won't believe that they're real and some will actually fear them. It's human nature that some will go on a quest to find out who put them there before they'll open the box and others will wish to have a book written on the best way to open the box. Still others will simply open the box, since it was obviously a grand gift with their name on it and 'see' the splendour of the potentials of the new tools.

Chapter 12

Matthew and Neil married and started families of their own. John and I built a house in a coastal town north of Perth and by the end of 1986 we'd settled into our new surroundings.

One Saturday night, not long after moving in, we went to the local social club where a three-piece band from Perth was playing. The company was great and we sang along to some of the tunes with Duncan, the lead singer.

Afterwards we stayed behind to help clean up, and driving out of the car park later we heard a loud metallic crash at the side of the club house. John turned the car around and in the headlights we saw Duncan standing behind his car, looking down, scratching his head.

We got out of the car and hurried over to him. "What's up mate?" John asked.

Duncan shook his head. "Beats me! Looks like I must have backed into that," he said, pointing to a low brick fence nearby, "and hit the muffler."

We followed his gaze, expecting to see his muffler bent or dented, but the impact had ripped it clean away from the car and it sat mangled on the ground.

"You've got a problem there, pal," John said, somewhat superfluously.

The other band members had left for Perth, the manager had just gone home and the club was locked up.

"Well mate," said John, "We can't do anything about this 'til morning. Looks like you'd better come home with us." "I guess you're right," he said. "Thanks for the offer."

The next morning John made several phone calls, but nobody in town could supply a muffler. Being Sunday meant the mechanic from the local garage couldn't order one from Perth until the next day, so it looked as though Duncan would be with us another night or two.

We had plenty of time to chat, and to our surprise we learned that he once met Wayne at a friend's home where they had a music session. He was older than Wayne – maybe forty or so – with a family of his own. He knew Wayne had been murdered and was upset and sympathetic when he learned he was our son.

I was really surprised when he said, "Sometimes we can't see any meaning in tragedies like this, but I believe everything happens for a reason, even if we can't see it at the time."

Since moving away from my group, I hadn't come across anyone who spoke what I'd come to call 'my language,' and when I heard Duncan talk in this philosophical way I felt the urge to have a deeper discussion with him.

That night, John, now a fisherman, went to bed early because he had to get up at 4.30am. As Duncan and I sat in the lounge room I said, "We haven't lived here very long, Duncan and I haven't found anyone in town I can talk to about certain things."

"What kind of things?" he asked.

"Well, I need to sort out some spiritual stuff in my life."

Right away he said, "I know just the person who can help you. My Mum."

"Fantastic! Where does she live?" "Over in Melbourne."

"Oh…"

"But hang on," he said. "We can phone her now if you like. She'll still be up. She doesn't go to bed 'til the early hours of the morning."

"But you don't even know what's on my mind," I protested.

"It doesn't matter," he said. "If it's anything to do with spiritual stuff, she'll be able to help you."

I looked at the clock. It was already 10.30pm. With daylight saving it was 1.30am in Melbourne.

I shook my head. "No, I wouldn't like to ring her this late, Duncan."

"Okay, if you'd rather not, but I know she wouldn't mind." Then he jumped up and said, "Wait a minute! I think I've got a letter from her somewhere."

He went into his room and came back with an envelope. "Here," he said, handing it to me, "Have a look at this and you'll get an idea what she's like."

I didn't like to read someone's personal mail but Duncan was insistent, so I took out the letter and opened its pages. It was its length – about four big pages – that took my attention right away because I, too, wrote long letters. Also, it was typewritten and contained numerous underlined words, brackets and explanations – as well as mistakes.

"Gosh, Duncan," I said, "At first glance this could pass for one of my own letters. I always type mine. And underline. And use brackets." I looked at him and laughed, "– and make plenty of mistakes."

I turned the envelope over and read 'Amie Cole,' with the return address.

"I don't believe it!" I said. "Her name's Amie too!"

Duncan smiled and said, "Yes. Interesting, eh? So let's see if you can do some of the things she can do. For instance…" He gazed at the ceiling in concentration for several moments before continuing. "She's got a rocking chair. Can you tell me the kind of pattern that's on it?"

"I'll try," I said. I laid my thoughts aside to allow the impressions to come to me and I could see a rocking chair, but it definitely had no pattern. "All I can see is smooth rounded wood."

"That's right," said Duncan. "There *is* no pattern on it. It's just round and smooth like you said."

I was quite surprised and couldn't help feeling pleased with myself, because I hadn't tried to do anything like this outside of a group environment.

Duncan had another question for me. "Mum's block runs downhill to the street. What's in the front of the yard near the fence?"

I thought of trees; ornaments; a letterbox. What could it be?

I tuned in again, then received an image of a fence, but couldn't see anything near it. I was sure he had me this time. "Nothing," I said lamely. "I can't see anything at all.

There's just the grass running down the yard and then there's the fence – a kind of wire fence." "Right again."

"Oh really?"

Duncan nodded and smiled. Then he asked, "So what kind of things do you need to sort out?"

I lowered my voice in case John overheard me. "It's hard to explain. I'm trying to find some information about something that's happened to me."

"Look, I have to tell you I'm not too good at this stuff yet," he admitted. "I'm just a beginner."

I let out a sigh.

"I'll tell you what I'll do," he said. "I'll ring Mum as soon as I get home and tell her you're going to be writing her a letter. How does that sound?"

I was more than pleased. "It sounds pretty good!" I said. "Thanks, Duncan."

Smiling, he said, "Things turn out the way they're meant to and like I said earlier, I believe everything happens for a reason. By the looks of it, you've got my muffler to thank – or rather, my bad bit of driving, eh?"

Chapter 13

In my letter to Amie, I briefly mentioned that Wayne had been killed and my premonitions before his death. Then I told her in detail about that very first meditation, describing the 'presence,' and how I'd learnt to control the lost souls that had previously almost taken over my life. I also explained the foreign language that was always at the ready. I closed by saying, 'I've been told by a few people that I'm having these experiences because of my psychic abilities opening up and I've tried to be happy with that, but I just don't seem to fit in anywhere.'

Within days Amie's friendly five-page reply was in my hands. As promised, Duncan had told her I would write. She greeted me warmly, saying she was delighted to offer her help. Next she gave details of a chakra meditation and described a method of white light protection, adding, 'Try it for about a week and then let me know how you're getting along. Remember the saying: it's our *intent* that's essential. It doesn't matter which way the wind blows, it's how we set our sails that determines our direction.'

I counted myself very lucky to have found such a person to guide me and started the meditation that very night. It seemed there was more than one way to use white light, for I'd been taught by Val and Sue to imagine myself surrounded by white light. However Amie's technique was to breathe the light in through the crown chakra until it filled me from head to foot. When I began her procedure I immediately became aware of the familiar buzzing of my crown chakra, then after only a few seconds I could feel a gentle wave of something close to euphoria throughout my body. In this sensitive condition I was wary at first about focusing on the chakras in case I encountered trouble from interfering energies, but thankfully my fears were unfounded. After about ten days I wrote and told her of my success.

As before, her reply came swiftly. 'That's great, love,' she wrote. 'Stay with it and you'll soon see things changing in yourself.' Then in the next paragraph she said, 'I'd like you to tell me about Wayne. How old was he Amie? And how did it happen?'

I didn't want to answer that second question and wished she hadn't asked. Firstly, I didn't feel ready to tell her the details and secondly I thought she might not want to help me if she knew the truth. My memory went back to about five years before Wayne died, when one day I was waiting for a meal at a take-away restaurant. To pass the time I was chatting casually about the weather with the man next in line when he pulled a small photo from his wallet and showed it to me, saying, "This is the only photo I've got left of my sister. She was murdered six months ago. I've been looking for whoever killed her, but I'm not having any luck so far."

I took a slow step backwards away from him, hoping it didn't look deliberate and mumbled something like, "That must be terrible."

I could see he was waiting for me to say more, but his words had put me on edge and my mind was blank. I grew increasingly uneasy and was pleased when my meal was ready so I could escape from this man, for I wanted nothing to do with his drama.

My quandary now was, if I told Amie what she wanted to know about Wayne, would she avoid me – and feel as I did when I hurried to get away from that man.

In the end I told her only that Wayne was nineteen and hoped she would leave it at that. But clearly she was not to be put off, for she asked again in her next letter, 'How did it happen, love? How did Wayne die? I need to know all about it before I can help you.'

Furiously I crushed her letter into a ball and tossed it in the waste paper basket. She was trying to make me say things I couldn't say; talk about something I'd only briefly spoken of to others. She wanted me to lay my wound bare and I didn't want to do it. I wanted her to *know* about it in case his death was somehow responsible for what had happened to me, but I didn't want to discuss it in *detail*! However, it looked as though no matter what I thought, this was what I would have to do to get the help I needed.

Reluctantly I retrieved the screwed-up pieces of paper and smoothed them out on my desk. Just the thought of putting the ordeal into words brought the memories and feelings flooding back, and I swiped angrily at my tears as I typed what I thought would be my last letter to Amie.

First, I wrote of how Wayne and his friend Jim had gone missing and then I said, 'They were both murdered. With an axe.' I thought she might as well have it all, and I kept writing, 'They were killed in their sleep and the man who killed them buried them on his farm. They weren't found for two months.' There. That was it. As I posted that letter I was sure I'd never hear from her again.

To my utter amazement, a week later I received a seven-page reply. 'I'm so sorry for your terrible loss,' Amie wrote.

'I can't begin to imagine the pain you and your family must still be suffering after such an ordeal.'

Further down she said, 'I'd like you to ask to see Wayne every day during meditation. He'll be shown to you in such a way it will leave you with no doubt at all it was him. Once you're convinced he's all right you'll begin to see light at the end of the tunnel. Believe me, Amie, you only have to ask.'

I was floored. Everybody *knew* such a thing could never happen, didn't they? I already knew in my heart that somewhere, somehow, he was okay and that was enough for me. I couldn't see any sense in trying to do something I thought was impossible.

Eventually I resigned myself to doing as Amie asked, simply because I knew she meant well and was trying to help me. I wasn't optimistic though and didn't think my half-hearted attitude would impress 'them up there.'

I did the chakra meditation first and then asked to see Wayne, but soon I ran into a hitch and turned to Amie for an answer. 'Nearly every day I see myself in the centre of a stage,' I wrote. 'And people rush in from both sides, pick me up and throw me around like a rag doll!'

'That's all coming from your subconscious, love,' she replied. 'It's been the boss all your life, doing as it pleases and now you're trying to bypass it and it doesn't like it one bit! All you can do is keep on the way you're going and sooner or later it will give up – but you must persevere. What you're doing with this meditation is oiling your rusty doors so to speak. Any of this type of picture that you see needs to be relegated to the back room and in time you'll leave them behind. When things begin to develop, believe me, you'll *know* the difference.'

For several days I doubted Amie's advice because those people still appeared regularly and kept throwing me about on that stage. But once I got the hang of it and learnt to show no interest, the visions faded and I was able to concentrate on asking to see Wayne.

Nothing happened until more than a week later, when I saw a picture in my head of Wayne and Neil talking together. I quickly sent a letter off to Amie detailing what I'd seen. 'Was *that* it?' I asked.

'No, darling, that *wasn't* it,' she replied.

Some days later I saw a beautiful angel and a circle of pulsating light, and Wayne came floating down through the circle. 'Was *that* it?' I asked again, wishing she'd say it was and I could give up this impossible task.

'No darling, that *wasn't* it,' she repeated patiently. Damn!

Meanwhile, Amie's letters kept coming, and were always filled with stimulating information that left me wanting more. I thought I'd be a fool to jeopardise such a vital link with someone so willing to help me and, for that reason only, I persevered with my assignment.

Sometimes I saw fleeting glimpses of Wayne and once I thought he touched my cheek. But each time, Amie said the same thing, 'No darling, that wasn't him.'

Boy, I was beginning to tire of this futility! Always the same answer: 'No, darling, that *wasn't* him.' Well, how would *she* know? After all, she'd never met him, or me for that matter. How could she be sure I hadn't seen him?

A noise woke me; it sounded like a human noise, like someone groaning. Where had it come from?

I listened for a moment. Nothing. John was still asleep beside me. I looked at the luminous clock on the bedside table – 2.20am – then drifted back to sleep.

The same noise disturbed me again just minutes later. Then again soon after that. When I heard it for the fourth time, I was roused enough to realize that the sounds – straining sounds – were emanating from deep within my own throat! As this realization hit me, my eyes sprang open and I quickly turned onto my back. If they wanted to tell me something worthwhile, they had my full attention. But if they were just mucking about I was ready to put up a fight and tell them to nick off and leave me alone!

Seconds passed. Then a wisp of pale blue haze rose ever so slowly from halfway down my body. As it wafted higher it took form – human form though featureless, like a store mannequin. My eyes were wide and unblinking as I watched hair, facial lines, skin tones, eyes as well as eye colour appear, then a smile formed and I saw that it was Wayne.

After about ten seconds he was gone and I realized I was lying there with my mouth open. John still slept soundly.

I went over the amazing episode in my mind trying to preserve every detail. Then, with sudden clarity, I recalled Brian's words of several years previously: '…You will be shown your son quite, quite clearly.' This, surely, was what he foretold.

But what would I say to Amie? Would she tell me again that it wasn't him?

I slid quietly out of bed and went to my desk in the spare room where, using pen and paper in case I woke John with the typewriter, I wrote down what I had just seen. When I'd finished, I could scarcely believe what I'd written. How could I expect someone else to believe my story?

The next morning, I turned my notes into a typewritten letter to Amie and, wanting to pre-empt the possibility of rejection, I added, 'I'm not certain that it was Wayne, but it sure looked like him.'

Several days after I posted the letter, the phone rang. "Hello Amie. This is Amie," said a lively voice.

"Amie! I don't believe it! It's great to hear your voice at last!"

She sounded excited. "Same here darling, but listen, I've got your letter about Wayne and I've got something to tell you."

The big smile on my face caved in. I was certain she was going to tell me it wasn't Wayne I'd seen, so I said dourly, "Okay."

"It's all right love. You don't have to ask to see him anymore! He showed himself to you by way of a re-birth so you'd believe it was him."

I tried to take in her words. "What do you mean 're-birth?'" I asked.

"The straining sounds you were making were those of a mother in childbirth and then when Wayne first showed himself, as you said, from half-way down your body, he was being re-born. He knew he would need to give you solid proof and that was it! You see darling, I told you – all you have to do is ask."

For a while I was walking on air, but it wasn't long before my excitement wilted as doubts came pouring in again and then even Brian's words lost their impact. I tried so hard to convince myself I'd experienced a miracle, but I just couldn't do it. The sounds that had woken me that night were real; I knew what I'd seen and yet the information wouldn't slot into my brain anywhere to make it valid. Amie's explanation made perfect sense, but I was willing to brush it all aside because, deep down, I couldn't really believe it.

John's mother and I had been writing to each other regularly over the years and recently her mother, Nanna Garvin, had died. In Mum Templeton's most recent letter she'd said, 'I miss Nanna so much and keep thinking of all the things we did in our lives. But she was in so much pain and hated being in a wheelchair, so I guess she's better off where she is.'

As I answered this letter, I found myself writing, 'I'd like to tell you something, Mum. I've seen Wayne so I know we don't die and your mum is okay.' The words were written with confidence, but was I trying to convince Mum Templeton – or myself?

Soon she wrote again. 'I know what you're talking about and I believe you, because I've already seen Nanna Garvin and before that I've seen Uncle Oscar and Uncle Gus and Auntie Eva. I usually see one or the other of them in the middle of the night.'

I could hardly believe what I was reading and thought we were heading for a stimulating discussion. Mum Templeton had always been a down-to-earth-no-nonsense kind of person and I had no reason to doubt her words. Next time I wrote, I asked, 'Would you like to tell me some more about it?'

'There's nothing to tell,' she answered. 'I just get annoyed with it most of the time. Why do I only see *dead* people?'

On one hand, I was greatly disappointed because it didn't look as though we were going to have that interesting talk after all, but on the other hand, I was amused by her line of thinking. Not wanting to hurt her feelings, I thought carefully about how to answer her question. 'Well Mum, they're trying to show you that they're *not* dead and that we *don't* die. If you were shown *live* people it would be missing the point.'

I was trying to help by answering her question to the best of my limited ability, but the ring of truth in my own words hit me like a ton of bricks and right then I knew with certainty, and was able to finally accept, that I'd seen Wayne.

Chapter 14

"I don't know if you can help me, Amie," said the voice at the other end of my phone. "My name's Karen and my boyfriend Leo is a friend of your son Matthew."

"I'd like to help if I can, Karen," I said. "What's the trouble?"

"They both suggested I come up and see you and have a talk. I'm having trouble with psychic things happening to me."

Matthew had obviously mentioned my interests, as well as my problems – what he knew of them – to Leo and Karen. I didn't know if I was able to help another person, but since Karen was willing to travel a couple of hours to see me I was happy to give it a try. "Well, I'll do what I can, Karen," I said. "When could you get here?"

"How about tomorrow afternoon?"

The timing was good. John was leaving on an overnight fishing trip in the morning. "Sure. How's 2.30?"

From the moment Karen arrived I questioned my decision to see her. We'd only just had time to say hello before a horrified expression crossed her face and she pointed to my gold Buddha on a shelf. "That's evil!" she whispered hoarsely. Next she pointed to a small statue of Kwan Yin and repeated, "And that's evil!" Then I followed her gaze to a wall plaque of zodiac signs as she declared, "And *that's* evil too!"

I was mesmerized and could only look on.

"Evil comes in threes," she said emphatically, "and my minister taught me that it can easily be detected when you know how."

Rarely did I hear the word 'evil', but Karen had just said it four times in less than a minute!

She covered her eyes with her hand. "I can't *bear* to look at that Buddha!" she cried dramatically. "Please take it away!"

Without a word I took it from the shelf and put it in my bedroom, closing the door when I came out.

It astounded me that Karen didn't leave at once, since, in her mind, she'd found such iniquity in my home, but when I suggested I put the jug on for coffee she seemed happy to stay. Then, over our steaming mugs she told me her story.

"Six years ago when I was twenty-four I had a vision one night in bed. Even though the room was dark, I could see a human shape and it told me telepathically that 'they' were going to take my husband Joe away from me. The shape said Joe would be fulfilled and contented where he was going and asked me not to be sad. I told my mother what happened, thinking she'd be able to explain it to me, or at least be able to help in some way, but she just said I was mad. A week later Joe put a shotgun in his mouth and committed suicide."

I couldn't hide my disbelief. "Oh! No!"

Karen put her head down and tears fell into her coffee. I went to her side to comfort her but she pushed me away. "No!" she cried. "I'm *evil!*"

I was Stunned by her reaction but as I went back to my chair I tried to be sympathetic and said, "You're not evil, Karen." Then I waited as she composed herself.

Calmer now, she pushed her long brown hair back from her tear-stained face and went on, "Joe had these two friends and about three months after he died, I could see these friends dead too! And two weeks later they were both killed in a car accident. I know I'm responsible. It was as though I'd wished them dead!

"After that, I couldn't make any sense of the bedlam in my mind and in my life. I would 'see' something, then it would happen – though nothing was ever as bad as the deaths of Joe and his friends.

"When I couldn't stand it any more I admitted myself to a mental hospital, but when they couldn't help me I went to a church and told my story to the minister." She took a deep breath. "He said I was evil! He said the things that had happened were evil! He came to my house and pointed out things – like an expensive cross and a big book of astrology and said they had to be burnt."

We sat there for hours, with Karen talking and me trying to reassure her. But it was plain she'd convinced herself she was evil and I couldn't break through the wall she'd built around herself.

We snacked on cheese and cracker biscuits and when we realized it was 4 am, she accepted my offer of our spare room for what was left of the night.

Our many hours of talking had left me completely exhausted and I sank into a deep sleep, too tired to make any sense of the thoughts that were trying to get my attention.

When I crawled out of bed the next day, Karen was already sitting at the kitchen table drinking coffee. I squinted at my watch. "What time is it? Is that 9.30?"

She was looking into her coffee as though she hadn't heard me. I pushed the button on the jug. "What about we go for a walk after breakfast? It's only two minutes down the track to the beach."

"Yeah, okay," Karen said dolefully, "then I'll have to get going."

For a while we walked along the water's edge, carrying our sandals, not saying much. Then, as we sat on the soft white sand and looked out across the ocean, Karen began talking in a monotone.

"While I was in that mental hospital, I told the doctors I was causing all this stuff to happen and that I wanted them to help me. But they just thought I was a great joke – said I was mad and kept me on medication.

"Other patients were doing strange things, like putting a second pair of shoes over shoes they were already wearing – that type of thing. It took a few weeks before I realized that because I was aware they did these peculiar things, I myself must to some degree be normal and I signed myself out. I promised to keep taking the medication and I took it for a while until it dawned on me I was in a stupor all day long; then I threw all the tablets away."

She looked at me, then back at the water. "I've tried to tell my story to anyone I thought might listen – my mother, friends, people at the hospital – but they all said I was evil and that I was going mad. The minister was the first one who tried to do anything to help. I know there's something wrong and I keep praying to God, but he hasn't helped me."

My thoughts from the previous night were beginning to come back to me. This time they were coherent and it was dawning on me that there were similarities between Karen's situation and my own, even though the details were different. She had a 'problem' and while to her it was unsolvable and very painful, I, as an outsider could see it from another viewpoint and the answer was simple – she was just psychic and didn't know it!

Here in front of me was the living example I'd spent years searching for in books! Karen was another person just like me, who was experiencing the pain and confusion of spiritual ignorance.

Compassion rose in my chest and I felt an overwhelming need to say to her what others had said to me. I tried to choose my words carefully. "You and I know you're not mad, Karen. And I know you're not evil. In fact, it's plain to me that you're psychic." There was no immediate reaction so I ventured, "Have you thought of finding out more from other sources about what's happening with you? You could start with some easy meditation...."

"But my minister says meditation's evil!" she shouted. "And I know I'm evil too and he's trying to get rid of the evil presence in me."

I was baffled. If she was happy with the help she was getting from her minister, why was she looking for answers from me? Even though she thought she wasn't technically mad, it seemed she *wanted* to believe she was evil! I didn't have enough knowledge at that time to be absolutely sure of my conclusions, so I stopped short of saying I thought she'd been brainwashed by her minister. It wasn't until after much more study that I became convinced my feelings were correct.

As she left at lunch time she said, "Until I met Leo and Matthew and now you, I'd never found anyone who didn't tell me I was evil. So, thanks for your time, but I don't believe what you're saying. I think the three of you are only patronising me."

I was lost for words.

Chapter 15

My encounter with Karen caused me to do some deep thinking. For one thing, I now understood that the reason I'd overlooked the truth in solutions that people like Sue and Val had offered was because I didn't know enough about the subject. Also, Jan had assured me I wasn't mad and my sister Maree didn't appear concerned for my sanity when she said she thought I was developing 'gifts.' More recently, Amie had said, 'All you need is guidance and you'll be able to see more clearly. Reach for the top of the spiritual tree first and you'll find what you're looking for.' Now, looking from the outside in, as I had with Karen, made everything so much clearer.

I was feeling pretty smug after putting those thoughts together, for in my mind I'd achieved great knowledge and my confidence levels went through the roof. My waking moments turned into a single-minded search for answers and I knew I was changing – not always for the better. It became a nuisance to take time out to cook a meal. I'd previously been fastidious with housework, but now I only skimmed the surface to give an appearance of tidiness. I was pushed along by a sense of urgency and wanted each new piece of information to bring instant understanding of all things knowable. I wanted Enlightenment, nothing less!

I thought that people who weren't aware of the wealth of knowledge available to them needed a wake-up call and I felt a desperate need to shout my eye-opening discoveries from the rooftops. Why couldn't people see things as I now saw them? What was wrong with them? It was hard for me to talk to 'ordinary people' or do 'ordinary' things and I wasn't interested in socialising except for the occasional outing, because I didn't seem to fit in – or didn't want to. Fortunately for me, this phase didn't last more than about six months, but I didn't realize until much later that it had a name – 'spiritual arrogance.' No wonder I was lonely.

* * *

As I continued to ask Amie many questions, she lent me some of her books, or sent new ones for me to build my own library. In this way I became acquainted with the wisdom of many thinkers. I wished I could just hold these books and know their contents and such was my hunger for information that before finishing one book I'd begin reading another – sometimes reading three books at a time. My education spread through such diverse areas as Eastern Philosophies and different ancient texts, the importance of the Mayan Calendar, which has an end date of the year 2012, Atlantis, Lemuria and other lost civilizations, and subjects not of this earth, including the possibility that we could be of extraterrestrial origin. The idea that I could be an 'alien' seemed a bit over the top at the time, but I became engrossed in the study of every one of these writings and wondered how I'd existed without them.

J.J. Hurtak's *The Book of Knowledge: The Keys of Enoch,* was mentioned in several books, so I bought a copy. That was a mistake. Without a doubt, I'd jumped in too early, because all I could understand in this remarkable tome of over six hundred pages were the prologue, introduction and parts of the glossary.

One day I asked Amie how she would describe God and she made it sound so simple when she explained 'God is a force, like gravity and is everywhere at the same time.' Sue had told us at her group that God was 'in everything,' and while that expression caused me to think deeply I couldn't quite grasp it then. In a flash the comparison of the God Force with gravity produced for me a crystal-clear mental picture, and as my mind accepted this concept I understood why I could never come to terms with the religious belief that God was a Being somewhere 'out there.'

I learned that the majority of religions were formed because their founders had an enlightening experience. Unfortunately many of the original details were obscured through teachings that later developed. As a consequence of different interpretations of religious texts, each belief system now considers itself to be 'the' path. I respected most religions, but had always felt that their structured walls would not reveal the answers to my questions. As Mahatma Gandhi once said – 'God has no religion.'

In *The Spirituality Revolution,* David Tacey quotes Karl Rahner as saying, 'The Christian of the future will be a mystic, or he or she will not exist at all.'

* * *

Amie never tired of my questions and her supply of new material seemed inexhaustible. She often reminded me that if I didn't like something she was sending, to toss it out or put it aside until later and she would find something more suitable for my present needs. But I found only joy in every letter or package I found in my mailbox.

Sometimes an expression that seemed insignificant turned into a vast and elusive subject – for example, 'living in the now'. My first understanding of this concept came when one day Amie wrote 'Try to picture this: As each thought leaves your mind it becomes a ribbon that takes part of your consciousness with it. Can you see that your consciousness would be weakened by this? Now, in your mind, roll up these ribbons of consciousness and bring them all back. When you do this your consciousness will be whole and strong once more – you will be 'centred,' which means you will have all your energy 'here'.

'Living in the Eternal Now' doesn't mean that we are never to think about the past – but we need to make those visits free of emotion. We can only reach our potential if our energy isn't constantly concerned with the past or what the future might bring. This is non-attachment. This is being 'in the world but not of it.' There is richness of life waiting when we learn to live in the NOW.'

Chapter 16

When Wayne was killed, we thought his death would protect us from another tragedy, but we found it doesn't work that way.

"Mum, we've just lost Brendan!"

"What?" His words didn't make sense. My grandson Brendan was only seven months old. How could he be lost? My mind was spinning. "What do you mean Matthew? What do you mean you've lost him?" Then it hit me. "Oh no! Don't say what I think you're going to say!"

Matthew's voice was breaking up. "Yes, Mum. He died last night. Cot death."

Paralysed by the news, I slumped onto the lounge. I can't remember what I said next, except that we'd get there as soon as we possibly could.

John and I arrived at Matthew and Angela's house to find them sitting motionless on the front verandah. They stood up when they saw us approaching, their faces reflecting the pain they were feeling as we held each other silently.

On the day of the funeral, the sight of Brendan's tiny white coffin was too much to bear. We all wept for Brendan, for Matthew and Angela, for our family and for ourselves.

* * *

I wrote and told Amie the sad news and when the phone rang some days later I answered it mechanically.

"Oh, you poor loves," Amie said sadly. Her voice was comforting. "I'm so sorry for all of your family."

"It's not fair." I said wretchedly. "Why did he have to die? He was only a baby!"

"Are you really asking, darling? Or are you just wondering."

"I guess I'm really asking. But I'm not expecting an answer."

"Well, what would you say if I told you that Brendan would have known before he was born that he only had a short time on this Earth," she said. "It's all planned out – although in very broad brush-strokes - before we come here."

If anyone else had told me this, I would have laughed at the idea, but hearing it from someone I trusted had my heart leaping because it seemed we were about to begin a new and exciting subject. I had to calm myself as I tried to work out what to say next. "When you say, 'before we come here,'" I said thoughtfully, "You must mean that we're somewhere before we're born."

"Yes, that's true." she said. "And it all depends on your views on reincarnation as to how you see this."

"Reincarnation? Oh…"

What a let-down! I'd already come across the subject several times of course, but couldn't fit the pieces together, so the ideas were still wandering around lost somewhere in my 'too-hard basket.'

"Yes, love, there are many things that can only be understood when you see them from a different perspective."

"Oh dear," I said wearily. "I'll have to work on that one Amie."

Even though I understood, so far, that we positively do not die, I still hadn't considered what happened to us or where we went when we leave our body. Now, apparently, I also needed to think about where we are *before* we're born.

When I researched the subject of reincarnation, it turned into an enigma with words such as 'holographic universe' and 'parallel lives' cropping up. I began to understand the meaning of a phrase I'd read, that the secrets of the Universe were almost unfathomable with our limited physical brain. My own brain seemed close to burn-out and I had to settle for taking mental notes, hopeful that the answers would come with time.

Chapter 17

John was watching cricket in the lounge room one Saturday afternoon and I went to the bedroom for a nap. I was lying on my back, nearly asleep, when suddenly the whole room, including me, exploded into a luminous golden-yellow brilliance. I was filled with aliveness – an energy – and in an instant I was in flight, looking down over rooftops and trees. The exhilaration was unbelievable, though my vision was slightly blurred and I couldn't recognize my surroundings. As I moved effortlessly through the air, I continued to radiate the glorious golden colour and my body was making a noise and vibrating, as though it was some kind of motor. After a short time my speed slowed and the next thing I knew I was back in my house, hovering in the bedroom. I could hear the sound of the television, which made me think of John and I hoped he wouldn't come into the room just then, for I wondered just what he'd see!

With those thoughts, I was once again lying on the bed, but my left leg had overshot the mark – it was somewhere to the left of my physical leg. A bizarre sensation indeed! I realized I'd been doing something called 'astral travelling,' and was able to remain calm because I remembered reading that temporary misalignment is possible if we return to the physical body too quickly. It took only seconds for the leg to float back into place and then the orange glow vanished and the motor noise ceased.[7]

---

[7] Astral Travel, or Astral Projection, can be referred to as 'out-of-body experience,' and is the conscious separation of the astral body from the physical body, such as many people report following near-death experiences. They describe seeing, for example,

About a month later I'd been in bed asleep for a couple of hours when I became suddenly aware I was halfway to the ceiling. I was being lifted from my bed by two beautiful beings who wore long white robes and whose flowing hair fell below their shoulders. When we reached the furthest corner of the ceiling, I looked back to the bed where John was sleeping and asked the beings telepathically, "Do you think I should tell him what's happening?"

To be honest, I didn't *know* what was happening, but I felt so blissful that wherever they were taking me I was happy to go.

They replied, also telepathically, "No, it will be all right."

Then it struck me that I was wearing my nightgown and I said something I've regretted ever since. "I don't think I'd better go any further because this is the first time I've been anywhere with you and after all, I'm only in my nightdress."

In the next instant, much to my extreme disappointment, I was back in bed beside John, who was still sleeping peacefully.

During the next couple of years, there were other episodes of leaving my body, but none with the golden colour and no beings were present.

These experiences, because they were personal and not something I'd read in a book, took away any thread of doubt I might have been harbouring that there is more

---

surgeons operating on their bodies and can recount conversations that took place when hospital staff thought the patient had died. Some have even brought back startling information that was not known to them before that time and sometimes this can be the result of a 'walk-in' – but that's another subject.

to us than our physical bodies. In more recent times I've sometimes woken to find my body vibrating and making the motor noise that accompanied my first astral journey. Whenever this happens I feel I've just returned from somewhere, although I have no memory of the trip.

Something different happened one night when I was thrust into wakefulness by an explosion in my head. My eyes snapped open and right in front of me in full colour was a face. I'd been reading *When Daylight Comes*, Howard Murphet's biography of Madame H.P. Blavatsky – and this was her face! I tried to hold onto the vision to see what else might happen – if anything – but the face had already begun to fade and after only about five more seconds it was gone.

I turned over to see if John had seen or heard anything, but you've guessed it – he was sound asleep.

* * *

Amie was still sending an abundance of material and I'd begun looking for repeats or similarities from different sources that, in my mind, confirmed pieces of information. By putting details together in this way the bigger jigsaw puzzle began falling into place and my view of the universe and our existence became broader. I still couldn't see where I fitted in but that other world was becoming increasingly familiar to me.

At some stage my focus had changed. The foreign language and other 'presences' had taken a back seat. This meant that while I still believed I was suffering a form of psychosis, I was no longer totally consumed by that possibility.

As time moved on Amie said, "I don't know why I keep getting the feeling I need to hurry and help you love. It's as though I'm being pushed to do it; as though there's not enough *time*."

Only weeks later, just before her seventieth birthday, she mentioned that she wasn't well, but still continued sending me, as she said, whatever she thought was appropriate. I enquired about her health, but she just said she wasn't feeling well and didn't give me any details of her illness. I assumed she had a bout of 'flu.

On the morning of 1st July, 1990 her husband Paul phoned to tell me that Amie had been admitted to hospital. "The prognosis isn't good," he said, "and they're going to do some tests."

I was shaken. "Do they know what's wrong?"

When Paul spoke again, his voice was choked. "They think it's her liver," he said, "but they won't know anything for some days. They said not to phone her. She's too ill to take a call."

Like Paul, I was heartbroken. I rang the hospital a few times and left messages that I'd called. The only other thing I could think of was to send her a card – a pitiful expression of the true depth of my feelings.

Amie died of liver cancer three weeks later. Oh, how I felt the pain of losing my friend.

Even though we'd never met we'd become so close over the past four years. She'd turned my life around by showing me the necessity of concentrating on higher things; of aiming for the top of the spiritual tree. In one of her letters she'd explained, 'Our psychic gifts are a natural product of spiritual unfoldment, just as roses are natural to the rose bush. If we think we've found 'it' when rosebuds begin to show, we might never realize there is a much higher potential. We need to work our way to the top of the bush and then, when we look back, we will see that we have all the 'flowers' we could wish for.'

I felt lonely – almost abandoned – without her guidance. I had yet to learn the difference between being 'lonely' and being 'alone.'

I knew I still had hard work in front of me as I searched for the elusive Enlightenment. As far as I could see, I had 'set my sails'. What more could I do?

Chapter 18

Late in 1996 we moved back to Perth, where I found that book stores seemed to have changed noticeably. Dymocks and Angus and Robertson now had well-stocked sections of spiritual books – and yet, maybe they'd been there all along and I hadn't known what to look for. Other specialist bookshops seemed to have popped up all over the city and suburbs, but I guessed I'd previously been ignorant of their existence and they'd probably been operating for years. Anyway it felt great to visit these shops and mingle with people who spoke my language as well as sold books and other items that helped with my continued search.

Right now, the icing on the cake was my discovery in one of these shops of a free newspaper that advertised courses on various modes of healing, iridology, hypnotherapy, spiritual development and contacting our guides – as well as other subjects I can't now recall. I was swept up in the excitement of it all and signed up for everything that caught my eye,

However, after each class, workshop or course I felt disappointed even though I'd succeeded in either obtaining the certificate, contacting the guide, or giving messages from 'the other side.' I expected bigger revelations *right then*! But it was never the case and I always came away looking for more.

Because of this lack of satisfaction, I rarely put my certificates to practical use afterwards, or focused on other psychic elements that I'd studied. Amie had said psychic gifts were a natural part of our unfoldment and I understood the truth of her words, and so I longed to find a way to fast-forward myself, but to where, I didn't know.

I was in this impatient and frustrated frame of mind when I went to see Charlene, who advertised that for over thirty years she had been helping people open their 'third eye'. I knew by now that the third eye chakra between the eyebrows was the pineal gland, which linked the physical and spiritual worlds. This centre is crucial to spiritual development and even though I couldn't understand how it could be activated by another person, I was still keen to investigate the possibility. No point leaving any stone unturned!

Charlene was tall, fair-haired and about my age. She greeted me cordially and I was happy to find that she was bright and energetic, which hopefully meant she was also good at her work. Without preamble, she led me through some lengthy visualisations, which I took to be an introduction to the main work – whatever that would be.

In one of the exercises, I climbed some stairs in bare feet. "I want you to tell me what the steps feel like," Charlene instructed. "Are they smooth or rough? Damp or cold? What are they made of?"

I didn't need to think about it. "They're damp and cool," I said. "And they're rough because they've been cut out of rock. They've got tiny grains of sand or something on them."

"The wall beside you is made of rock, too," she said. "Is this wall on your right or left?"

"It's on my right."

"I want you to touch it with your fingertips and nails and tell me what that feels like."

In my imagination, I felt the wall. "It's cool too, and it's got sharp pieces on it. When I scratch at it with my fingernails, I can feel something like bits of moss."

"The stairs open onto a rooftop," said Charlene. "Is it day time or night time?"

"It's day time."

"And what's the weather like? Is it raining? Fine? Snowing? Cloudy?"

"It's cloudy."

Similar exercises followed and finally she said, "Okay, you can open your eyes now."

I wondered what was going to happen next and as I waited expectantly she smiled and said, "Your third eye is working very well. It doesn't need any help at all."

I felt let down. This meant I wouldn't get to see how it was done. I was also very confused. "Oh, is it? Doesn't it?"

"You just need to work with it some more," she said.

On the way home, I wondered if my third eye was really open. If so, could this be where the pictures came from when I gave those messages to people in the group? I had no idea what my third eye being 'open' was supposed to be like. Was this how it was when you gave it a name? Maybe, just maybe, she was right. My too-hard basket was beginning to sag.

A week later, I was chatting with Doreen, a participant at yet another workshop, when I learnt of something entirely new.

"I've just started doing 'past life' readings," she said. "I don't know where the information comes from but I *do* know it's not coming from me," she confided, "so I trust it and go with it."

"Hmmm. That's different," I said. I wasn't really interested because it sounded complicated, but still I asked, "How do you do it?"

"First you need the person's permission. Of course, if they ask you to do a reading, you automatically have their permission. But it's not right to practise on people without them knowing about it." With the class about to begin, she quickly added, "Get their name and birthday. The rest is easy. Just ask!"

With the course behind me, I started thinking about my conversation with Doreen. She'd talked of her venture into the field of past lives as though it was an everyday event, like trying a new brand of tea. It didn't sound too complex after all, but the concept created a quandary for me because it was clear there could be no past lives without reincarnation, which was a subject I was still struggling to accept. I finally came to the decision that the only way to see if there was anything to learn from these readings was to try them for myself.

Doreen and I had exchanged phone numbers, so I called and asked if she would like to be my first volunteer.

"What a good idea," she chortled and gave me her surname and birthday.

"Thanks for helping me out," I said. "I'll let you know what I get."

Sitting at my kitchen table, I protected myself by breathing white light into my body and asked for help from my highest guides. Then I wrote, 'Would you please give me a past life reading that is relevant to this life time for Doreen,' and gave her other details. Doreen had said, 'Just ask.' I remembered that those were Amie's words too.

With my pen poised, I tuned in.

I waited patiently and soon, in the same way as for inspirational writing, sentences started swirling through my head. One by one, I grabbed at the words and wrote them down until, after a little while, I could 'see' nothing more. As I examined the mere half page of writing, my emotions alternated between feeling failure and success, for even though the information wasn't well structured, somehow I could easily put it together and 'knew' how to fill in the gaps.

I phoned Doreen and, deciphering my notes, I began, "Well, I don't know if this means anything to you, but the information I've been given says that in another life you were a Chinese man and used to have a Chinese spiritual teacher."

Doreen interrupted. "Of course, you haven't been to my house, have you? You should see the Chinese stuff I've got here!"

"Oh really!" I said, pleased she could identify with the theme.

"Sorry to interrupt. What else?"

"The teacher was tall and slim and wore mainly red and gold Chinese dress. You used to take regular lessons in a special room in his very large house. Or it could have been a temple of some kind. There were beautiful decorations on the walls, like banners with Chinese writing on them. Over near a window was a big wooden table and this was where you both sat to do your lessons. Each time you arrived, the teacher went to a carved chest on the floor in the corner of the room and took out one of many scrolls. He would teach you for several hours at a time from this scroll, and when he came to its end he selected a new one – and so it went on. And that was all I could get."

Doreen sounded thrilled. "Gosh, for a first attempt, that's good!" she exclaimed. "It helps me to understand why I'm drawn to collect Chinese items," she said. "I also have a Chinese garden."

"It doesn't tell much about the rest of your life though," I said. "I hoped I'd get more information."

"If I were you I'd be very pleased with what you've been given," she replied. "You'll probably be given more information once you get used to it."

Chapter 19

It was only through idle curiosity that one day I asked for a past life reading for myself and wondered if I'd be told John and I shared a previous life together. I received the following:

'The one known as John is handicapped – crippled from an accident. The one known as Amie spends her life looking after him. Even though she knows he would regain strength more quickly if allowed to do some things for himself, she feels the need to wait on him constantly and believes he will still become stronger eventually. It gives her pain to think of him struggling to tend to his own needs and she never wakes to the truth – that she is responsible for him remaining forever in a weakened state.'

I thought this reading was, at the least, interesting, because I found it rewarding to wait on anyone who was in pain or ill and I wondered if there was a time when I'd overdone it. Also, if the words were true, they pointed towards John and me being together previously. But because the information wasn't conclusive, I filed the writing away and thought no more about it until several months later.

Meanwhile, still looking for volunteers, I phoned Maree. "Do you know anyone who'd like me to do a past life reading for them?" I asked.

"I sure do," she said. "Me!"

I purposely hadn't asked Maree if she would volunteer. Being my sister I was concerned my own thoughts would probably intrude and not allow for an unbiased result.

Nevertheless, I said, "Oh, good. Good. And will you see if you can find someone else for me too?"

"I'll ask around and let you know."

The next morning, a little reluctantly, I commenced the reading for Maree. At first I received words in my head the same way as previously, but when I'd written just one line I could see moving pictures. I also began to feel emotions that I was able to associate with the scene before me. I still received words as well – just not as many – and they helped to describe the scene. This is what I received:

'You were a little black girl – so black your skin shone – and you were very pretty. You were about six years of age, lived in Africa and were called a piccaninny. Your hair was in little curls and you were wearing a red dress, though it could not easily be recognized as red because it was very grubby and worn.

'You were sitting beside a small muddy stream and had one foot in the water. Someone came up from behind you and lifted you under the armpits and took you in their arms. It was your mother. She was a huge woman. You almost disappeared into the folds of her body. You said nothing and neither did your mother. You were both weak and very sad. You were also very hungry, but there was no food.

'There was a noise from somewhere behind you. You sensed your mother's panic as she turned towards the disturbance. Men were cutting a path through the jungle towards you. These men were led by your father, who had banished your mother and you because you were a girl. He had wanted a son.

'He had thought you were both dead, but had recently heard that you had been surviving by travelling between other tribes, staying only a short while at each location. His humiliation had overwhelmed him and now he had tracked you down with intent to kill you both.

'Your mother ran with you in her arms. She found it hard to maintain her footing on the slippery mud beside the stream, but managed to make it to a darkened area that was sheltered by many intertwining trees overhead. She put you down and you stood very close to her, just about hidden by her voluminous skirt. Even though you were clinging to her, all fear had left you because your hunger was the only thing you were aware of.

'Your father and the other men had followed your mother's footprints in the soft mud and were now coming closer.

'Your mother scooped you up in her arms once more and started running again, but as she did so, she slipped on the mud and fell into the water, hitting her head on a jagged jutting rock. She landed on top of you and both your head and hers were under the water. You were unable to free yourself from underneath her heavy body. You both drowned there, hungry and alone.'

I sent Maree a copy and in reply she wrote, 'Thanks Wen. First of all, I can't wait for you to tell me how you did it! I think it's really interesting.' Then she continued, 'A few things came to mind as I was reading. From as far back as I can remember I've always had a fear of water. Then one day at the beach, when I was still very young, a girl jumped on me and held my head under water. She wouldn't let me up and I panicked. I thought I was never going to breathe again and I was fighting for my life. A relative finished up having to rescue me and the feelings of terror are still with me today. Another thing is that I must say I do like my food and find it a real comfort. I think I use food to compensate for not having enough at some time.'

I hadn't known about Maree's fear, or her awful experience of having her head held under water, so my reading about her being drowned could not have been influenced by any pre-knowledge. I was, however, aware that she liked her food, but it hadn't occurred to me to connect this knowledge to the reading.

"By the way,' she added, 'A friend of mine, Simon, would like you to do a reading for him," and she gave me his details.

For Simon, this is what I received:

'You were a Spanish sailor on a ship with many sails. Your life was fast-moving and exciting. Your captain was a good man and you were happy to serve him. This was to be your last trip, as you were soon to be married and thought it was time to retire to the land.

'Your ship was returning to Spain after trading with far-off islands. You had been many weeks at sea and even though you loved sailing, you were looking forward to seeing your homeland and your beloved once more.

'You had been off duty, sleeping, when you heard the cry that another ship was in sight. When you raced to see for yourself, it was obvious that the other ship was not friendly.

'The sea was rough. The waves were high. Yet the other ship cut perilously close, forcing your captain to take evasive action. Your ship rolled dangerously and the deck was awash. You held tightly to ropes and a mast, but just when you were thinking all was well, the other ship cut in close again.

'It was a bigger ship. More stable. Now that it was closer you could see it was manned by pirates and they were trying to board your ship.

'The sea was foaming and conditions made it impossible for the pirates to manoeuvre. They sailed away, but it was too late for your ship to be saved – it had taken too much water.

'As it sank, you were still clinging to the ropes and mast. You could not believe that the end of your life was coming. You had put off doing many things back home in Spain because of your love for the sea, but now, just as you had decided to settle down and begin these projects, you knew they would be left undone. Also you would never marry – would never have children.'

I sent a copy of the reading to Maree, who passed it on to Simon. Later she phoned me with some feedback. "He was very happy with the reading," she said. "He said it helps him to understand why he's always felt so grateful for his family and felt such love for them. And he's never without a project to work on – especially his boat."

I continued doing these readings whenever I was asked and soon there was another change in the method of receiving. This new transition gave the material more substance and now, after information about someone's past life was transmitted to me, I received an explanation of how that life was relevant to events in the person's present life.

It wasn't always smooth going. Sometimes I broke a connection because I could see up to three different stories at once and didn't know what to do with the confusion of information. Whenever this happened, thoughts of parallel lives hovered in my mind.

* * *

John had returned to truck driving when we moved back to Perth and at about 9.30 one morning I received a phone call from Joondalup Hospital that I'll never forget, telling me that John had been seriously injured at work. His left shoulder had been torn from its socket when a piece of concrete weighing three hundred kilograms fell from the truck he was unloading. As I raced to the hospital after hearing this terrible news, the past life reading of John being crippled kept flashing through my mind.

While John only stayed in hospital for two or three days, the following weeks were filled with endless medical appointments. His neck and back had also been injured in the accident and he was in constant pain. With that reading now at the front of my mind, I had to continually remind myself not to smother him with attention.

Eventually, after several months, he had an operation to reconnect his shoulder, but unfortunately the use of his arm did not return immediately. It was more than three years before he was able to return to light work and even now he suffers severe pain.

It would have been so easy for me to wait on John night and day, but would I then have been responsible for leaving him in a 'weakened state' for a second time? I guess I'll never be certain, but it's food for thought.

During John's convalescence my quest necessarily became less frantic, and it was during this slower period that something different came my way while I was doing a favour for a friend.

Margo was a delightful eighty-eight-year-old lady who lived just around the corner from me. We'd met at one of the courses I'd attended and now I sometimes took her shopping or to medical appointments.

Margo suffered severe headaches and nothing she tried brought any relief. One day she handed me a leaflet. "Do you think this man would be able to help me Amie?" she asked. "Would you have time to take me to see him?"

The flyer showed a photo and details of a healer, Marcus, a born-again Christian, who would soon be setting up a tent in our area for a week. I wasn't very interested in going, but because it was Margo who was asking I answered cheerily, "Yes, of course we can go. He looks okay, doesn't he? You never know, he might just have what you're looking for."

"I haven't been to that kind of healer before," Margo reflected.

"Neither have I," I said. "It'll be something new for both of us."

"Would you mind if Norma came with us? I've been talking to her about him and she sounds interested." Norma was Margo's friend who lived not far away.

"No, that's fine," I said. "I'll be happy to take you both."

We arrived punctually for the 10am meeting on the first day and when I peered inside the giant-sized tent I couldn't believe every seat was empty. An untidily dressed man, unsmiling and unshaved, was standing at the entrance. When I read his name-tag – Marcus – it was hard not to show surprise, for he looked a far cry from his refined photo in the advertisement. Margo and I glanced quickly at each other.

As we walked inside, we were approached by a man and a woman who handed us some brochures. At least these people were neat and tidy.

Margo's hearing wasn't good, so we sat in the middle of the front row. A short while later, two more women and three young children came in and sat about three rows behind us.

By ten fifteen, no more people had arrived and Marcus, looking annoyed, left his post by the door, walked to the lectern and opened his Bible with a flourish. As soon as he began to speak, it was obvious he had a heavy cold. "Where are all the good people, the true believers, from this area?" he boomed. "Are they still home in bed? Why aren't they here? I thought this place was full of Christians. Where are they?"

His tirade was continuous and I shrank in my seat, wanting to leave right that minute. He reminded me of my father shouting at us in a drunken stupor when we were children. I whispered to Margo and Norma asking if they'd like to leave, but they shrugged their shoulders and indicated they were happy to stay for the time being.

Marcus ranted and waved his arms in the air, sniffing and wiping his nose with the back of his hand all the while. "None of the Buddhists or Hindus or anyone from those other religions will be going to heaven, because they aren't born again," he yelled. After a slight pause, he followed with an accentuated "AMEN!" He paused again, looked at us and bellowed louder, "AMEN!"

Seconds ticked by as we waited for him to continue. Then, arms extended towards us, he raised his hands palms up and, in a voice that nearly brought the tent down he screeched, "AMEN!"

At long last, I understood that he wanted us to repeat "AMEN!" I heard a meek 'AMEN' or two and even muttered one myself.

"You won't go to Heaven if you aren't born again and you are to believe ONLY in Jesus. AMEN!"

Again, unenthusiastic sounds came from the meagre audience.

"NOBODY goes to Heaven unless they're born again because it says so in the Bible. AMEN!"

Silence.

He gave up on us with the AMENs, but then pressured each of us about where we went to church. Well, as it turned out, none of us attended any church at all and this *really* set him going. He came from behind the lectern and leaned over us. "How do you expect to get to Heaven if you don't even go to *church*?" he roared. Then he looked at us each in turn and sneered, "Do you think you're Christians?

Are you born again?" I was wearing my cross and a crystal and just then they caught his eye. He pushed his face close to mine and leered, "What are you, a Spiritualist or something?"

I immediately pulled away from him and he made a huffing sound and went back to his lectern. I chuckled to myself despite my misgivings. The man had to be an idiot. A quick look at Margo and Norma suggested they agreed, for even though Margo was holding a handkerchief to her mouth, her laughing eyes gave her away. Norma simply laughed out loud.

I spoke to them out of the side of my mouth. "Do you want to go?"

Margo whispered, "How can we go when we're having such fun!" and we all giggled like schoolgirls.

I turned to Marcus and said boldly, "Yes, I'm a Spiritualist." This wasn't the right name for my beliefs, but what did it matter what he thought?

He turned his head with a dramatic, haughty swish and gazed off into space, then, still facing away from us, said slowly and sarcastically, "That's nice."

I could feel myself getting angry with this person who professed to be a healer and a Christian. "We're not here to be ripped to pieces by you," I said loudly, making sure he heard me. "We only wanted to listen to you and have a healing! We're still happy to do that if you'd just get on with it instead of criticising us for our beliefs!"

He glared at me for a full ten seconds and then suddenly flipped through the pages of his Bible in frenzy. When it seemed he'd found what he was looking for, a satisfied smile touched the corners of his mouth and in his typical theatrical fashion, he quoted a section on how the Spiritualists pretended they wanted to learn, but in fact only wanted to discover what the healers knew so they could do it themselves.

I couldn't believe what I was hearing.

When he finished reading, he launched a full-scale attack on everyone present, saying we would never go to Heaven. Then he lashed out at one of the ladies behind us. "You've brought a negative situation with you!"

"No I haven't," she answered curtly.

"Yes you have! You're full of it! It's showing all around you. It's been spreading to everyone else in this tent!"

"There's no negative situation with me," the lady insisted angrily. "It's just in your weird mind!"

A scraping of chairs followed and I looked around to see that the ladies and children were leaving.

Marcus watched them until they were some distance away and then said to his helpers, "Well, that gets rid of the demon. Now we can get on with this meeting!"

That left just the three of us in the front row and I could hear Margo and Norma making groaning noises that told me they were now ready to go. I gathered up my belongings and was about to stand up, when Marcus commenced another assault.

"What does it mean to be born again?" he demanded to know. Then he turned to me. "Who's the only person to believe in? What happens when you die? Answer me!" he shouted. "Answer me!"

I was speechless. His bullying was inexcusable and I'd changed my mind from thinking he was just a fool to believing he was insane.

When we didn't reply, he leapt from behind the lectern and put his face near mine, spitting droplets all over me as he gleefully tried to answer his own questions. Disgusted, I grabbed a tissue from my bag and wiped my face. Then as we all stood up in unison, Marcus threw his Bible down with a bang on a nearby empty chair – there were plenty of those and said heatedly, "Well, this is the end of this meeting! I'll be teaching you no more!"

We got out of there as fast as we could and went straight to the nearest coffee shop, where one minute we were in fits of laughter and the next, expressing our disgust at what we had just witnessed. For a long time afterwards we remembered it as the day we were kicked out of the healer's tent.

I'm sure Marcus was one of a kind, because I know there are many genuine healers doing great work. This unforgettable event broadened my outlook considerably and reminded me of the need to be constantly 'discerning.'

Chapter 21

By this time I'd lost the urgency to study everything that came to my notice. I now had a clearer understanding of different aspects of spirituality and had proved, to the best of my ability – and if only to myself – that each facet had substance. However it was the few spiritual truths I'd uncovered that really spurred me on and I knew I'd barely scratched the surface.

Months passed, and as I explored the writings of new authors I began to understand that once we've discovered we are spiritual beings we might often be alone, but we are rarely lonely. With this realization my heart went out to lonely people throughout the world, especially those who felt lonely in a crowd as I had once been. Many of these people believe there is nothing to live for and without spiritual awareness they will endure sadness for the rest of their days.

Although I didn't see the changes until they'd taken place, I was able to accept people that I mixed with just as they were, without expecting them to share my beliefs. I recognized these changes as positive signs that I was moving forward, growing, and I should have been smiling, but in the back of my mind I knew something was holding me back. I'd learnt to recognize the presence of lost souls and send them to the light, but I was no closer to discovering where the 'foreign person' belonged, or the reason for the 'presence.'

I'd been to different psychics, hoping to meet one who could 'see' my burden and either explain it or get rid of it. As I could never find the words to explain myself, I stared at them intently, willing them to look closer at me, to read me more deeply, to please help me. Some said I had 'much work to do.' Others said they could see I had many guides, or told me I had surprises in store. For me, these weren't answers and I went away downhearted.

Then one day I went to see Yvonne, who claimed she could sense the energies of a person's guides and produce them in a drawing. This was something entirely different for me and I was curious to see how such drawings were achieved.

Yvonne worked with assorted coloured pens and I watched and waited for a face to take shape, but after some time there were only coloured lines and swirls all over the page. Next, with her pens still moving, she broke out in a lather of perspiration and sounded flustered as she said, "This has never happened before. I'm always guided to draw a head-and-shoulders picture, or a whole person, but this time I'm just drawing energy. Does that mean anything to you?"

I frowned as I searched my memory. "Not really," I said, "But in all the meditations I've done that are meant to connect us with our guides, instead of seeing a person, I always just see a bright light. Do you think that means anything?"

"I'm pretty sure it does. You've got some powerful energies around you and I'm sure you'll find your path before too long."

It wasn't until later that I began to ask myself whether Yvonne's description of 'energies around me,' and the energies that felt like they were inside me, could be one and the same – the feeling I called a 'presence.' It's a shame she wasn't able to elaborate, because I felt she'd touched upon an answer for me.

I was strolling through a psychic fair in the suburb of Claremont some weeks later and felt drawn to Abbey, another psychic. Her sign nearby said she could see if entities were invading a person's aura, so I decided to let her have a look at mine.

When I sat opposite Abbey at her small table, I made up my mind that it was time to share – or maybe to shock! I wasn't looking for pity, so I tried to sound assertive. "I'd like to know if my aura is being invaded," I began, "because I speak this foreign language – it's like another person living inside me – and I don't know what to do with it or how to get rid of it."

'There,' I thought. 'I've done it!'

But you could have knocked me down with a feather when Abbey smiled sweetly and said, "I speak another language too. Listen." Then she moved closer and let loose a string of foreign words in my ear!

"Wow!" I said excitedly. "That's amazing." "Is yours the same?"

I shook my head.

"Would you like to speak it?" she asked.

I looked around at all the people close by. "No. I'd be too embarrassed. Mine doesn't come out easily like yours. I never know what's going to happen. Most of the time 'they' take deep breaths first and the whole thing can be very emotional."

"That's probably because you've been hiding it and fighting it," she said kindly. "How often does it try to come through?"

"Nearly every day. It's been going on for years."

"I know it'll work out all right in time," she soothed.

"In time!" I cried, forgetting about looking confident. "How many more years can I go on like this? How many more people do I have to see? Can't you help me?" I pleaded. "I need to know how to understand what's happening and what to do with it!"

"The best way I can help you is to tell you to *trust* in what's happening. It's part of you. Accept it and go with it – don't fight it. That's what I had to do."

I shifted uncomfortably in my seat and said despondently, "My 'voice' won't identify itself. Won't speak English. I thought I'd begun to come to terms with my situation, but now…" I choked on my words as tears stung my eyes and I knew I was a long way from being out of the woods. I asked, rather rudely, "Well, if you can't help me any more than that, can you tell me if there's anything clinging to my aura?"

Abbey looked at me intently for a few moments. "I can see lots of energy there, but there's nothing negative around you," she said. "So tell me more about what happens with you."

"Well," I sniffed, "in a nutshell, when I read my books, or even when I'm not doing anything specific, I can feel a 'presence,' like I'm not the only one there. I feel like a human pendulum the way my arms and head move on their own even when I'm just *thinking* something. I've been taught to control these energies, but they're never too far away. There were lost souls in there somewhere too at one stage. I'm fed up trying to work it all out. What am I supposed to do with it? What's the purpose of it? In twenty years I haven't been able to find the answers I'm looking for. I honestly thought I was coping, but now I realize it was all just a front!"

Abbey was unmoved by my outburst and just smiled. "I agree it can seem pretty daunting at the time," she said, "But I hope it will ease your mind to know that we're never given more than we can cope with. I can't prove it, but I'd like to convince you somehow that there's nothing wrong with you. Sometimes explanations are virtually impossible, but the fact is that provided our intention is good, then what happens to us along the way is also for our good."

She paused and looked me squarely in the eyes before continuing. "You'll be helping yourself immensely if you can be accepting and move on. You're holding up your progress because you've been trying to find explicit answers. Your experiences are all part of who you are. There's no need to listen to what happens with other people or to try to fit into their mould. We can't draw energies to ourselves that we're not ready for and what's happened *to* you is meant *for* you. It's different for everyone and that's why it's never easy when we're looking for answers."

I could think of nothing to say. There was a power in Abbey's words that exposed the truth I'd been unable to accept for so many years. It was as though I'd been chastised and given a beautifully wrapped present at the same time.

Then she surprised me with a question. "How would you like to see if there's anything wrong with my health?"

"Um, I'll try if you like, but why?" Abbey was younger than me – a robust-looking motherly type who didn't appear to have any health problems.

"I just know you can do it," she answered. "And I want *you* to see you can do it."

I was curious. "How would I go about it?"

"Just tune in to my body and go through it with your third eye."

I knew I needed to give it my best shot so I sat back and relaxed. After gazing at her for several seconds, I could see a picture of her liver. "Your liver," I said with quite some confidence. "There's something the matter with your liver."

"What else can you tell me about it?"

I could see a strip of what appeared to be fat lying along one edge, but was hesitant to mention it.

"It's all right," Abbey prompted. "Tell me what you're seeing."

"There's a layer of fat, I think, all along the left-hand side."

"Yes, you're right," she said. "And I'm on a very strict diet."

I was spellbound and still looking at her liver when she said, "Tell me what else you can see."

I shifted my focus and this time I saw her heart. "I think you've got something wrong with your heart," I ventured.

Abbey indicated for me to keep talking.

"I don't think this is physical. I think it's to do with a sensitive personal issue you're experiencing at the moment." I had no idea where the words were coming from. They were just simply 'there' in my head and I let them come out. "I feel there's something happening in your life and you have a very strong need to see it have a certain outcome, but if you can release this need, your heart will be strong again."

Abbey smiled at me. "Good. You're spot on," she said, "And as far as I can see, you've got nothing to worry about. I've often spoken to people who said they'd listened to one brilliant teacher after another, sometimes for years, before catching on that they weren't allowing the words to penetrate – to become a part of them. I think you're one of these people. We need to work with what we learn – to see the information as more than just words – before changes can be brought about. And when this transformation takes place, it reflects outwardly in our lives."

In that moment, I was hit with a wave of new understanding and the light finally dawned. She was right of course. For instance, I thought I knew that the God Force is in us all and that we don't die, but I only 'knew' these things at an intellectual level. Had I lived that knowledge, I would have reached out for help knowing the answers would come, not from a belief that I wasn't good enough. Our true Awakening can only occur when we take our hands off our life and stop resisting – when we 'let go and let God.'

In the months that followed, having allowed myself to 'trust,' the differences that were taking place on the inside were more apparent and I knew I was growing into the energies around me. I recalled how years ago I was able to understand Lobsang Rampa's *You Forever* when the time was right and at last a part of me understood the process of my own development.

Chapter 22

About a year after that memorable reading with Abbey, I was sitting in a café with a friend, Francesca.

"This course I'm going to take soon should be terrific Amie," she said. "It's a series of special meditations, and Ellen, the lady who runs it, is an old friend of mine. She gives 'knock-your-socks-off' healings, so the course should be out of this world. Why don't you come with me?"

I carefully broke open my warm, fresh muffin while I thought about it. I wasn't interested in doing another course. "Do you think I'd get something substantial out of it?" I asked uncertainly. "I know I need to go with the flow, but I don't know…."

Francesca cut in. "I think you'd be silly *not* to go. The meditations are channelled – they're different to the usual and will raise our vibrations. You've told me you speak a language. Well, Ellen speaks a language too, and you'd have something in common."

Ahh! That was different. Now she had my full attention. We both knew I hadn't yet found an outlet for my 'foreign friend'. I decided to be bold. "If I go with you, would you be able to tell her about me before the course starts?" I asked hopefully. "She might find the time to point me in the right direction."

"Yes, sure," said Francesca. "I'll ask her next time I'm talking to her. It starts in three weeks. The whole course is in two sections that are a month apart. Each section's made up of an introductory Friday night and full days on Saturday and Sunday."

"That sounds okay," I mused. "You'll go then?"

"Yes," I said cheerfully. "I'm looking forward to it."

On the first Friday evening we walked into the course venue in Fremantle at 6.30pm. Already there were seven or eight people of the expected twenty or more waiting for Ellen to begin at 7pm.

I mingled easily with the early starters, some of whom – like Ros, Louise, Wanda and Tom – said they'd completed a previous course and were back for more of the same. By the time everyone arrived and Ellen was ready to commence, I felt a bond with every person in the room.

Although petite and unassuming, Ellen immediately captured my attention when she said that we were now in a time when new teachings are emerging and that never before had the planet experienced such a spiritual awakening. She went on to explain that the meditations she would be taking us through would clear our chakras and bring us into alignment with our soul's purpose.

After her introduction, she led us through lengthy meditations for protection and for clearing imbalances in our physical bodies. By the end of the evening the atmosphere was one of light-heartedness and unity and it was easy to see why one would come back for more.

The next day, Saturday, and again on Sunday, the meditations rolled on one after the other, each with a different, higher purpose.

As the weekend came to a close, Francesca called me aside. "Ellen said if we wait back she'll talk to you about the language."

"Oh, great!" I said.

When Ellen had said goodbye to the other members of the group and locked the door, she pulled up a chair to where Francesca and I were sitting. She smiled contentedly and said, "What a lovely weekend." Then she turned to me. "Francesca tells me you'd like some guidance about the foreign language that you speak."

"Yes, that's right. It's been with me for many years and I'd like to know how I'm meant to be using it."

"I'd like to hear it then. I can't promise anything, but I'll see what my guides tell me."

"Sounds good to me," I said. "It might take a minute for me to bring it through though. I've suppressed it for so long, it'll probably wonder why I'm trying to encourage it after all this time."

"That's okay," said Ellen lightly. "We'll wait." Then we relaxed and closed our eyes.

About fifteen seconds passed before I felt the shift of energy throughout my body that I'd come to recognize as the onset of a state of light trance. Tears welled behind my closed eyelids, followed by laboured breathing and a pounding heart – then, out poured the language we'd waited to hear. The flow stopped after about half a minute and my consciousness returned to normal.

As I opened my eyes I saw Ellen's eyelids flutter, then she spoke for several seconds in a foreign language that was completely different to mine. When she'd finished she said laughingly, "Well, at least we know they're not the same." Then she went on in a more serious tone, "I'm being told you've got two more languages waiting to be expressed."

"You're joking!" I spluttered. "Two more? You mean they're waiting to come out *now?*"

Ellen gave me a smile. "That's what they're telling me."

I became confused and anxious, looking from Ellen to Francesca, then back to Ellen. "So what do I do? I don't know what to do! What do I do?" I knew I was talking too fast.

"Just relax and let's see what happens," Ellen said calmly. Francesca smiled in agreement.

They seemed unperturbed, but my mind was agog, trying to imagine what would happen next. I'd spent years trying to either unload or come to terms with just *one* language. It was unthinkable that now two more were about to emerge. I tried to relax and just waited.

Within seconds I was again in a light trance, but the tears didn't come and my breathing remained close to normal. I was startled when my solar plexus began heaving rapidly and with each spasm-like movement unusual sounds were forced from my throat. My initial concern dissolved to be replaced by intrigue as I tried to decipher these new sounds. The nearest I could guess was that they were like the sounds made by a dolphin or a whale. Then, abruptly, those sounds stopped and as my solar plexus came to rest, I listened, fascinated, to the clicking noises my tongue was now making and I started speaking in a completely different way. Next, the original language returned and when it stopped after only a handful of words, I knew the communications had come to an end.

For the second time I returned to normal consciousness, feeling as though I was waking from a dream, for even though I knew what had just taken place, it was hard to attribute any reality to something so extraordinary. It felt as though it was happening to someone else.

Both Ellen and Francesca looked unruffled and I waited anxiously for one of them to speak.

"I'm being told that these languages will be used for healing," said Ellen. "And most people will understand at a soul level. Some will laugh. Some will cry. But whatever it is that they do, a healing will be taking place."

I hung on her every word, not saying anything for fear of breaking into her thoughts.

"These are fragments of yourself from past lifetimes in other constellations that have found you and each other," she said. "You need to talk about it – to share it. You are yearning for your home and the emotion that comes with these languages is yours, not theirs. It's what *you're* feeling for *your* loss."

I went home in a daze. With the answers Ellen had given me, I knew that I'd reached some kind of life climax, but I was also besieged by another whole dimension of questions, like, did these languages truly belong to other parts of me parts that came from other star systems? Memories rose from the misty place in my mind that I still called my too- hard basket. Certain books I'd read several years previously such as Amorah Quan Yin's *Pleiadian Perspectives on Human Evolution* – had left deep impressions.

The common theme was that we all have galactic origins. At different times I'd also read detailed personal accounts by people who claimed to have come from the stars.

The second part of the course wouldn't be for another month and in the meantime I had lots to think about. The mystery that had plagued me for many years seemed to be solved, so did I want to take things further? If I did, by what means would I share my languages? It was beyond me and right then I couldn't even face the thought of continuing the course. I just wanted to put my head in the sand.

Chapter 23

I decided to complete Ellen's course mainly to satisfy a personal need to finish something I'd started, and when the time came to attend the second segment I soon felt at ease once again in the company of Ellen and the other participants.

The weekend was going uneventfully enough until we neared the end of a meditation on the last day, Sunday – and then something bizarre came over me.

I started shaking inwardly and dizzying thoughts flitted through my mind in a continuous speeded-up parade. I managed to open my eyes part-way, then tried to tell Ellen what was happening, but thought patterns slipped away and I couldn't join words together to make a sentence. In a stupor I gazed around at the others, but although I recognized the faces I couldn't remember anyone's name. Even though I was disoriented, I could see that a few people looked spaced out and some were crying.

Suddenly I was enlivened with an electric energy and, although it was similar to what I'd been experiencing for years, it was intensified to the point where I felt I might float away at any moment. Tears overwhelmed me – huge tears as though an immense grief was being expressed from cavernous depths within me. I was sapped of all strength and could not stop the profuse flow of tears or the sobs that racked my body. At least ten minutes passed before the energies withdrew sufficiently to allow me to gain some self-control, and I was very embarrassed at the spectacle I imagined I'd made of myself.

I wobbled to my feet, thinking I'd go to the kitchen and make a cup of tea, but I was too weak to walk. Seeing the trouble I was having, helpers quickly gathered around. Louise and Tom steadied me as I sat down again. Ros brought me a mug of tea and Wanda gave me a piece of cake. My words slurred as I tried to thank them, so I gave up and was sipping the tea when Ellen approached me.

"I think the reason this is happening to you is that now is the time and place you're meant to allow the languages to express themselves fully," she said. "Would you like to do that?"

I looked at Ellen and tried to focus, then said shakily, "I think so. It feels right."

Immediately the energies leapt into life again. My body jerked upright and I was in danger of dropping the mug and cake – until someone took them from my hands. In the background I could hear Ellen making an announcement. "…there are aspects of Amie that wish to express themselves and what is to be said will be for the good of everyone present."

By now my face was awash with fresh tears and I tried to silence the sobs that again shook my body. Efforts to compose myself were useless, for these emotions were coming from someone that was not me, Amie, as my conscious self.

In despair I called to Ellen, "I can't do this. He won't stop crying!" Then, sensing a strong energy above my head, I looked upwards and begged, "I can't do this if you won't stop crying!" Ellen reacted quickly by moving closer, her arms outstretched, with palms towards me to project healing energy.

There was no immediate change, but gradually the weeping eased and I was more in control of my senses. I closed my eyes and as tears dripped freely from my chin, the three languages expressed themselves one by one – sometimes with great vigour; at other times in gentle, rhythmic tones. Finally my eyelids fluttered open and through bleary eyes I could see that several people were crying and the atmosphere in the room seemed subdued.

The fog of my surroundings was clearing slowly, but even so I was unable to move for at least five minutes. Once again I was embarrassed, thinking I'd made a fool of myself, yet something told me that this incomprehensible event was meant to happen and that everyone present had been greatly affected. I felt loved and empowered, as though at long last I'd found where I belonged.

Ellen waited several minutes and then asked for comments from the others. Wanda, her face wet with tears, was first to respond. "I started to write what I was receiving from my guides while Amie was talking the languages," she said. "But I was overcome with emotion. I couldn't stop crying and I couldn't write any more."

Then several others spoke, some saying they'd been able to understand the words at some level and that the experience was 'uplifting.'

To help me remember the details, Wanda and Louise later wrote what they recalled after I first began to cry:

Wanda: *When the crying continued, I opened my eyes to see Amie's knuckles white from clenching the chair and her body was jerking. I could sense the strong energy around her.*

Louise: *We thought she was in a huge release process and needed support and encouragement emotionally and physically. She seemed fragile as she struggled to talk or hold her body upright. We know the realisations that come to us during these meditations can be profound and she had the support of the whole group.*

Wanda: *Ellen spoke briefly to Amie, then announced to us all that she, Amie, had a message to speak. Ellen suggested we close our eyes and hear what was to be said with our hearts, for it might be in a language other than our own.*

At first, the sounds came as huge, huge sobs and the energy in the room expanded. We felt surrounded by calmness and a surreal stillness. Her body shook with emotion as if an overwhelming sadness was being expressed. It felt like grief, despair and every human emotion you could name.

Louise: *We remember her saying, 'I can't do this. He won't stop crying.' Then she looked above her head and said, 'I can't do this if you won't stop crying!' She gained some composure and then the words began to flow. This was when the personality of the being she was channelling became apparent to me.*

I saw this and other beings as tall and robed, with an ancient oriental demeanour. They appeared to be honouring us in the same manner as the ancient traditions of these cultures, where sacred ritual and respect run deep.

Wanda: *The grief that had been expressed so strongly by the male energy changed to forceful, guttural sounds. This soon made way to softer, almost whispered words that seemed to be spoken by a second being. These words heralded peace and celebration and reverberated around the room.*

Louise: *When the beings finished speaking, Amie appeared exhausted, but she seemed uplifted too and all symptoms of distress had vanished. It was as though her task was complete. She appeared fulfilled and at the same time emptied of a burden she had carried for so long.*

Wanda: *Those in the group who shared their experience of the sounds spoke of peace, celebration and a mission accomplished beyond expectations. Nearly everyone said they were touched by caresses of love, which were felt, rather than heard and our hearts responded.*

About half an hour after this event that would be forever etched on my mind, I was badly in need of some refreshments. On my way to the kitchen, I saw Francesca sitting alone at the far end of the room and wondered if something was wrong. I walked over. "Are you okay?" I asked.

She jumped when I spoke and turned her face away, putting her hands up, palms facing me. "I'm all right!" she said quickly, unsmilingly. "I'm processing a lot of stuff at the moment. Please leave me alone."

The energies in the room were still very strong and we were each affected in different ways. It was easy for me to understand her not wanting company. "Okay, no worries," I said softly and continued on to the kitchen.

Later in the afternoon I thought I'd see how she was going, but when she saw me approaching, her eyes flashed angrily, so I went back to my seat. Something was still affecting her and I was concerned that she had so much to deal with. I didn't take her actions personally; nor did I consider for a moment that her anger might be directed at me.

I didn't start to think anything was wrong until I noticed Francesca had nothing much to say to me for the rest of the day – or even after the course had finished.

Then, about three months later, she sent me a long email.

I was anxious to know what she had to say and quickly started reading, but after the first few lines I couldn't see the point she was making. I scrolled through to the end, trying to gauge by her closing lines whether the communication had a positive or negative angle. I was relieved to see that it was positive.

> Hi Amie,
>
> I hope that what I'm writing makes some sense to you. Ellen's course has been a catalyst for many changes taking place in me. Until you and Ellen started talking in Star Languages, I had been totally unaware of different star system origins, or of galactic conflicts, wars and annihilations. I was so shocked at how strongly I was affected! The reaction in my galactic origin memories – as I came to know them to be called – created great discomfort and turmoil in me because those memories were so shameful. These feelings totally overshadowed the 'here-and-now' personal connection between you and me and I couldn't deal with what I was experiencing – that you and I were from opposing star systems. This was nothing to do with you personally and I

can only apologize if I upset you or caused you confusion.

I think my reason for writing this is that I believe you needed to understand why some people will accept your gift of languages happily and others will respond negatively. Whichever way they respond, it will create a space for healing – maybe not immediately – and you might need to tread gently and give people time for acceptance of their own healing.

You've been very brave and I honour your courage (not that you feel you have much choice) to follow your path even though you don't know where it is leading.

With love and thanks for the healing opportunity.

Francesca.

I replied with the following:

Hi Francesca,

Can you help me put your email into perspective and to understand more fully what you're saying?

I knew something was affecting you, but had no idea what it was. I didn't think I had done anything to cause you to withdraw and thought it best to leave you to work things through for yourself.

You said your memories were shameful. I believe that anything we feel is shameful is only so in our own minds. Also, thank you for the thoughtful advice and I'd like you to know that I would definitely tread very gently because I know of no other way, having tried to hide my 'problem' all these years.

What you see as bravery and courage is my attempt to find my way through the cobwebs. I feel anything but brave and, you're right – at the moment I'm still not sure what I'm meant to be doing or where the path is leading.

Love, Amie.

Francesca then replied:

Hi Amie,

Thanks for your patience in trying to understand me in the spirit I intended. I'd love to *try* to explain more clearly what's been going on in my mind. Can we catch up for a coffee?

Love, Francesca.

We greeted each other with an affectionate hug and a few tears when we met at our favourite spot the very next day. That meeting healed what had become a rift between us, but although we talked for more than two hours, when we parted we still hadn't been able to translate our thoughts and feelings of this astonishing event into something easily comprehensible. However, one point I had previously overlooked now made itself very clear and that is the unfathomable depth of healing needed for our soul.

In a way I was glad I didn't know Francesca had been experiencing such extreme turmoil, because my reaction would have been to shrink back not only from everyone at Ellen's course, but also from other people in my life. Being totally oblivious allowed me the necessary freedom to fully accept my own intense inner experiences.

A few months later when I found an advertisement for another meditation group, I felt an inner nudging to practise what I'd learnt. The address was quite a distance away on the outskirts of the city, but it felt right, so I phoned the number.

The next Wednesday afternoon, I followed Frieda's directions and knew I'd found the right place when I saw the sign 'Weddings – Funerals – Namings' at the front gate. The house was in a bush setting behind a magnificent garden feature of American Indians, a huge fish pond and water sprays. A couple of sheep wandered happily around the yard adding finishing touches to the tranquillity of the scene.

Frieda, tall and dark-haired, was warm and friendly and introduced me to the other six members of the group, who were either sitting in lounge chairs or lying on mattresses on the floor. After the meditation, three of the ladies, Eileen, Sandra and Danika gave everyone in turn an uplifting psychic message and then we all moved to the kitchen for afternoon tea.

Soon a couple of people began saying their goodbyes and I was disappointed because if this was the end of the meeting, then it seemed the group was only for beginners.

I was on my way to the door with the others when Frieda announced, "Right. It's time for the healing room. Who's staying?"

I was surprised when Eileen, Sandra, Danika and another lady, Gayle started down the hallway towards a different room.

So this wasn't the end of the afternoon! "Healing?" I asked. "Yes, I'd like to stay. I thought we'd finished."

"The reason for afternoon tea between the meditation and healing," Frieda explained, "is to give people a chance to leave if they want to. Most beginners aren't ready for the healing room."

"What a good idea," I said, as I followed her down the hall.

Frieda's healing room was just like others I'd seen when doing courses on the subject. Incense and candles were burning, crystals hung at the window and in the centre of the room was the healing table.

We took turns either standing at the table as a healer or being the 'patient,' and I was very quiet that first day, saying nothing much about my experiences.

As the weeks went by I became more relaxed, although I was happy to just listen as Eileen, Sandra, Danika, and sometimes others, gave messages to the 'patient' we were healing. Gradually I began contributing, but only with short messages. I thought it best to wait until the ladies came to know me better before allowing my language to come forward.

Once, when I was the 'patient,' feeling totally relaxed and enjoying my special time, I suddenly heard a high-pitched sound – like a soprano's operatic note – coming from someone in the room. It took me by surprise, but I kept my eyes closed and tried to figure out what it was and who was creating it. Then there was a short silence before someone – the same person it seemed – began speaking what I guessed to be an American Indian language and I recognized it as Sandra's voice.

When the healing session was over, I caught up with Sandra as she was leaving. I couldn't help myself – I had to speak to her about what had occurred. "What was the noise you were making?" I asked. "And how did you start talking that language?" I probably sounded blunt, but I was just excited.

Sandra didn't seem to notice my abruptness, "Well, it's a long story," she laughed as we sat on a bench outside Frieda's front door. "But it started with the 'noise,' as you call it. It's called 'Angel Toning' by the way."

"Oh thanks. I haven't heard of it before," I said. "How did that start?"

"My throat started hurting and I didn't know why. The pain wouldn't go away, but I knew I wasn't sick. Then one day, luckily when I was in the house on my own, I stood up from the breakfast table and out came this really strong sound. My mouth was hardly open and there was no effort on my part at all."

"Did your throat stop hurting?"

"Yes, but it was queer because the sound sort of by-passed my throat – it was coming from right down in my solar plexus. Still does. And now I just let it happen when I feel the urge for it to come out, otherwise my throat hurts. It usually happens at the healing table."[8]

---

[8] Trudie Moore, Sydney medium of many talents, says about Angel Toning, "When Channels or Shamans sing in healing sessions, it's from a place of compassion as wo 'step out of our own way' and allow the loving powers of the universe to work

I was enthralled. "And when did the language start to come?" I asked.

Sandra leaned against the back of the bench, looking thoughtful. "I believe that the toning opened me up for the languages – there's more than one. I was in a healing group at the time and there was a lady there who spoke a few American Indian languages. She was getting on in years and asked her guides to pass the energies of those languages on to me."

"When did this happen?"

"About three years ago, I think. After that, I woke up some mornings feeling as though I was an Indian. I could feel my long hair. Sometimes it was black and in plaits. At other times it was loose and at those times it was always grey and white."

"Unbelievable!"

"I bought a book one day and on the way home the Indians began chanting in my ears. This was something new and it quite startled me at first."

"I'll bet!"

"Anyway, I started reading the book and came across a part that talked about black magic. I hadn't realized the subject was in this book and wouldn't have bought it if I'd known. I flicked quickly through and found black magic mentioned a number of times. Then the chanting got

through us. We focus on being a conduit, an instrument and indeed, we feel 'played through.' Listening to Angel Toning sets up powerful energy fields that activate dormant stages of consciousness in the body. It allows us to transcend this physical world and remember our connection to the source to experience again the unity of the universe and heal pain and illness."

louder and I closed the book right away when it dawned on me that they didn't want me to read it. I knew I had to get rid of it and first of all I threw it on top of the wardrobe, right up the back. The Indian chanting didn't stop, so I climbed up and got the book down again. I knew I had to put it in the bin.

I took hold of it and – you won't believe this – I tore it in halves in one go! Like this!" She held up her hands and demonstrated a ripping motion. "The whole thickness of it. Then the chanting stopped."

I was amazed. "Go on," I said.

"After that I often heard the Indians chanting," she said. "But it was different, not urgent like that first time. I knew they were guiding me along the right path. I learnt to trust them, as well as trust myself and then the languages started coming through regularly at the healing table."

Just then Frieda opened the door and poked her head around the corner. "Want a cuppa?" she asked.

Sandra and I both looked at our watches and jumped up. Nearly an hour had passed. "Thanks, but I'd better get going," Sandra said.

I started walking towards my car. "No thanks, Frieda," I called over my shoulder. "See you next week."

Every week in the healing room I was encouraged to join in and not hold anything back, and at first I didn't receive much in the way of messages through the usual manner of tuning in. However now and again I became filled with energy in a way that was completely unfamiliar to me. Whenever this occurred, it was as though the energy itself spoke through me and delivered what later proved to be a genuine message from a departed loved one to the person on the healing table.

Also, my talk with Sandra seemed to have been the green light I needed to allow my main language to come through. In the beginning it was accompanied by the usual laboured breathing as well as tears, but over time the words slid out as easily as in normal conversation. It seemed the second and third languages were also trying to come out into the open as sometimes I felt spasms in my solar plexus and a few sounds came from my mouth. Also, occasionally I produced some words of the clicking language. Nobody seemed at all disturbed – only interested.

Monica and Joanne were friends and came along for the first time one Wednesday, and after the meditation I looked in Joanne's direction and could 'see' a picture. "I can see a tribe of people at the foot of some mountains," I said. "There are lights flickering here and there – fires I think. It seems to be a scene from a long time ago. Does that mean anything to you?"

Joanne shook her head. "No, sorry. Not a thing." I didn't think any more about it until later.

Being their first visit, I was interested to see that both these ladies stayed for the healing session. When it was time for Joanne's healing, the rest of us took a place around the table. I stood at her left side and when the usual quiet fell over the room and we began projecting energy through our hands, I started speaking the language that had by now become natural to me.

As my hands moved about above Joanne's body I began to feel an unexplainable tenderness towards her, and then I noticed tears rolling down the sides of her face. For some minutes I continued talking while she wept silently. When the language ceased and the others had completed their healing, we gave our usual thanks to the healing guides present in a simple closing prayer. Joanne had stopped crying and was resting quietly with her eyes still closed.

"Take your time getting up," Eileen said. "You might feel a bit light-headed."

Joanne nodded and opened her eyes.

I was concerned because she'd been so overwrought. "Are you all right?" I asked.

She started crying again. "They were killing my babies. Now I know why my daughter Chloe is so special and why I need to protect her."

I put a reassuring hand on her shoulder. "Perhaps we can have a talk about it later," I suggested.

She wiped her face and nodded again.

When she didn't return to the group the next week, or the week after, I worried that I'd frightened her away. Her friend Monica came along now and again, but four months passed with no word from Joanne. I started to let the doubts creep in again and one day, not really wanting to hear the answer, I asked Monica, "Do you think I scared Joanne away that day in the healing room?"

Monica looked surprised. "Oh no! Absolutely not. She's just been very busy doing a course at uni. She was really helped by that healing."

I was more than relieved to hear those words. "Do you think she'd still feel like having a talk to me about it?"

"I'm sure she would. I'll give you her phone number. I know she'd like to hear from you."

A week later, Joanne sat in my lounge room. "I thought I'd scared you away," I said.

"No way!" she answered firmly. "I've just been snowed under with my uni course. In any case, I was too emotional after the healing. I wouldn't have been able to talk about it. When you rang last week the timing was just right. I'm starting to feel a bit stronger now." Then she smiled. "You see, my daughter is so special to me. I've done enough spiritual searching to know she chose to be my daughter and I try to give her the happiness every day that I know she deserves. I nearly lost her during my pregnancy, but I hung on until just a few weeks before normal birth time. She was healthy when she arrived, but my husband Nathan and I split up a few months later because he said he'd give up the drugs when Chloe was born. It didn't happen.

"A couple of years after the divorce, Chloe went to stay with her father for a few days a fortnight, but she always came home saying her head hurt. I thought she was having headaches, until I found out that Nathan and his step-father had been physically abusing her by hitting her head against the wall. It turned out they were mentally and sexually abusing her too.

"I had to fight for two and a half years in the courts to get custody and then afterwards she and I came from Sydney to Western Australia to live with mum and dad."

I was anxious to hear the connection between this heartbreaking story and the healing, but I didn't want to pressure her and waited patiently. I was soon rewarded as her incredible story unfolded.

"When I was on that table, I was seeing pictures. First I could see mountains, then I lost touch with the healing room. It was summer time. I could see myself cooking breakfast over an open fire and the youngest of my five children was near me. I belonged to a tribe and everyone was wearing animal skins. It felt like I was really there.

"Then an invading tribe started attacking us, killing as they advanced, but the only thing I could hear was your voice."

I was captivated. "Was I there with you?"

"No, not physically. But I could hear your voice saying, 'It's all right. You're safe. I'm here.' I knew you were trying to protect me from those people. Then I saw them kill four of my babies with spears. I grabbed up my youngest and joined with the other women who were running for their lives towards the mountains behind us. Everyone was screaming and yelling and I could smell blood all around me. But I couldn't save my baby."

At this point Joanne started to cry and I could see she was living the experience all over again. She reached for some tissues from the box on the table in front of her and tearfully went on with her story.

"They speared me in the leg. I fell down and that's when they killed my last baby. They tried to take me away, but you somehow held me back and saved me. You were saying, 'It's all right. Come away now. It's finished. Time to go.' That's all I saw, then I drifted out of the picture and you were still talking. For the whole time the emotions were so very strong that I felt as though if the healing hadn't finished just then, I, as Joanne, would have died there on the table."

I had a lump in my throat and was struggling with my own emotions. "That's quite a story Joanne," I said at last. "I had no idea what you were going through."

Then, I again saw the vision that had come to me just before Joanne's healing. I could see the mountains and the lights flickering in the distance. A woman was lying very still, blood spilling from her wounds. I knew it was Joanne and asked her, "Even though you can't remember, do you think they killed you as well as your children that day?"

"Yes, that *is* what I think."

I was trying to let these implications sink in when she asked, "Can you tell me something?"

"Sure. Whatever I can."

"While I was on the healing table, I could hear you in the room, speaking a language that I couldn't understand. Then, when I went into the scene, I could still hear you, but the strange thing was that suddenly I could understand every word. I knew everything would be all right – that you were trying to help me and would keep me safe. And then, when I came out of it, you were still talking, but I couldn't understand you again. How does that sort of thing happen?"

I looked at her not knowing how to answer. My course with Ellen and those later talks with Francesca had shown me that different types of healing penetrate to the soul level, but I had no understanding of the mechanics of this delicate procedure. "From what I've learnt, it's our soul that understands and this is just the way it works," I said, knowing I didn't sound too convincing. "We can know that something amazing has happened and if we also recognize that a healing has taken place, I believe that's the main objective."

"All I know is that I was very strongly affected that day," said Joanne. "It's something I can't forget. Now I've got such a deep understanding of my relationship with my daughter and I know why I fought so hard with the courts so they'd let me keep her. So I'm really glad you phoned because, as I said earlier, I didn't think I'd be able to talk about that experience – to live through it – ever again. I feel so much better now."

* * *

I am very grateful to Joanne and previously Francesca, for bravely sharing their stories with me, because they allowed me an insight into the depths that can be reached during a healing. They also strengthened my trust in both the process and myself.

My experiences firstly with Abbey, then Ellen and Sandra, taught me that I was far from alone in speaking one language or more; that there are many talents available to us and a new dimension is always waiting to be revealed.

For me, one of those dimensions was closer to being discovered than I could have imagined.

Chapter 26

I first learnt about Craig when I overheard a conversation in our local shopping centre.

"I'm sorry but I can't make it to your barbecue tonight," one lady was saying.

"Why? What's wrong?" asked the other woman.

"My friend's sixteen-year-old son committed suicide and I need to be with her."

"Oh, that's so sad. When did it happen?" "Yesterday."

"Where does your friend live?" "Up in the hills a bit."

I walked on, leaving the conversation behind. But I couldn't get their words out of my head. I could relate to the range of emotions that losing a child can create and thought of the pain the family must be experiencing.

Over the next few days I felt an urgent need to contact those people to offer some comfort and support – to let them know I was there if they needed someone to talk to. I didn't know whether they would accept my offer but I had to act on my feelings.

It occurred to me that the reference to 'Up in the hills a bit' might mean somewhere near Frieda's place, so I gave her a call.

"This might sound strange, Frieda," I said, "but I heard of a boy who lives up your way who committed suicide a few days ago. I wondered if you might know the family. I'd like to contact them to try to help in some way."

Frieda lowered her voice. "I certainly do know the family. In five minutes I'll be doing the funeral service."

It would be a gross understatement to simply say I was amazed. It had to be divine timing.

"Oh, I didn't know," I said slowly. "Well, could you please pass on a message to them that I'd like to offer some help later on? I've just got this feeling that I need to do something…"

"Yes sure," said Frieda. "I'll let them know."

Later that day my phone rang. It was Frieda. "They'd be very happy to talk to you. Do you think you could come over tomorrow?"

At 10am the next day I was at Frieda's place looking over a display of belongings and photographs that were still laid out from the funeral. There was a banner that read, 'Craig.'

So that was his name.

"His parents and eighteen-year-old brother will be here in about ten minutes," Frieda said.

Suddenly – swoosh! – I became filled from head to toe with powerful energy. This was the feeling I'd sometimes experienced in the healing room, but now it seemed ten times stronger. Then, although it was still my voice, someone else began speaking through me – loudly and emphatically. "They called me and I had to go – RIGHT THEN! There was no time to tell anybody. I'm so sorry for all the pain I've caused. I love everyone very much."

Could this be Craig?

The talking stopped and the 'person' gestured in a lively manner towards the memorabilia, then walked backwards and forwards apparently looking at the different items and said, "Look at all this! This is great! I'm so happy with the way my stuff's been displayed. It shows how much they thought of me."

It *had* to be Craig!

I hoped the family would arrive soon so they could see for themselves what was happening. This experience was a startling new development for me and I had no idea how long I could hold the energy.

As if reading my thoughts Frieda said, "They shouldn't be too long now."

Craig appeared agitated and began walking from one window to another, looking out. He seemed to be waiting for his parents' car to turn into the driveway.

At last the family arrived and the sadness they radiated almost crushed me. It was then that I understood what such depth of pain looked like from the outside. Perhaps even more sadly, I'd previously met Craig's mum, Catherine, through a business connection. Although I didn't know her well, I imagined that seeing me in this different capacity would be causing some embarrassment in her vulnerable state.

Next, with my arms moving about in the air, Craig again loudly repeated the words he'd said earlier, "They called me and I had to go – RIGHT THEN! There was no time to tell anybody. They called me and I had to go RIGHT THEN. I'm so sorry for all the pain I've caused. I love everyone very much."

Then the intensity of Craig's energy subsided, and my language came through and gave the family a message. For the first time I was able to interpret the words, and the message was that Craig's death would bring about uplifting spiritual changes for the whole family.

Craig's dad, Martin, and brother Bailey seemed convinced that this message and the messages from Craig were genuine, but as Craig began to speak again I could see Catherine had her doubts.

Studying my face carefully she said, "Craig, I need you to prove to me that it's you."

But Craig's energy had subsided again and I felt helpless. "Catherine, this is me, Amie, talking now. Craig seems to have gone for a minute. I'm sorry, but I have no way of proving it to you. I can only give you what I'm getting."

She sounded distressed. "I need to know it's Craig. I need him to show me something to prove that it's him."

I had no idea what message could convince Catherine and was deeply concerned that the sign she had asked for would not/could not come about. Catherine would go away believing I was deluding her, but there was nothing I could do or say to change that situation.

Then with a sudden jolt Craig's energy returned with full strength and he began walking backwards away from the family.

I started feeling dizzy and nauseous. "I'm feeling odd in the head and I feel sick," I said. "I think I'm going to faint." Then I thought to ask, "Did Craig ever suffer this kind of problem?"

Martin answered quickly, "Yes!"

I began shakily walking further backwards. I stumbled. Frieda and Martin moved closer and as I started to fall they caught me before I hit the ground.

Craig said loudly, "See, this is me! This is me!"

As they helped me up Martin said, "Craig woke up dizzy every morning – it was something to do with blood pressure and nobody outside the family knew about it."

A little while later he explained more fully. "Craig had been struggling for about eighteen months with headaches and low blood pressure. He couldn't get straight up out of bed in the mornings – he had to wait until his blood pressure was right or he would get an instant headache and be dizzy. We had an MRI done, trying to work out his health problem and he was on prescription medication for his headaches. They thought he had nerve damage in his neck from a motorbike accident but they had it wrong." Then he added, "You've been using the same expressions Craig would have used, and the mannerisms are the same too."

Then, I could 'see' a staircase. "Do you have a staircase in your house?"

The three of them looked at each other, then turned to me and nodded.

"Did something happen there?" I asked.

Martin said softly, "Craig hanged himself on the staircase."

* * *

It's almost two years since Craig's passing and these are some of Catherine's thoughts:

> After Craig's funeral Frieda said there was a lady called Amie who was anxious to have a talk with us, so Martin, Bailey and I agreed to meet her at Frieda's place the next morning.
>
> When we arrived Frieda told us that Craig was able to speak through Amie and that she had a message for us. I found I'd met Amie although I didn't know her well and I wondered what this older person could really have to offer.
>
> After a little while of talking with Amie, Craig apparently came through and slowly wound up. The whole scene was hard to comprehend. The emotion was huge and as she waved her arms around she kept rubbing her chin just like Craig and she was talking very loudly, saying, 'I'm sorry, I'm sorry, I'm sorry, I had to go, they were calling me and I had to go. I love you, I love you all.'
>
> Next she was bowing to us and started talking in tongues. Then she explained that the message was from the higher spirits telling us that even though we wouldn't understand now because our pain was too deep, the experience of losing Craig would uplift all our lives.

Then she went back to being Craig and I searched her face, desperately hoping I'd see something there that would prove this was my beloved son talking. I said, 'Craig, I need to know it's you. I need you to show us something that will prove it's you.'

Amie started telling me that Craig had gone for now, but then almost right away she began walking around in a weird fashion saying she felt dizzy, then she collapsed and said something like, 'Well, this is me.' They helped her up and Martin told her that Craig had a problem with his blood pressure.

When I went home I found myself analysing everything. Was it really him? I still wasn't convinced. I asked myself, 'Do they tell you what you want to hear?'

Being a grounded realist I'd hoped that it could be him but still had my doubts.

In the time since Craig's death, I've come to a much better understanding of the spiritual world and I now have a lot of respect for what took place that day with Amie. Since then I've found a doorway that opened my eyes and led me to a place where hope exists and nothing happens by coincidence.

I've read every book I can get my hands on to try to understand about life. When you start to switch on and pay attention there's just so much to learn.

I believe Craig would be beside himself with frustration because it's taken me so long to accept that he is living in another dimension that we just can't see. I can hear him saying,

'For crying out loud Mum, how much proof do you need?'

I'm slowly opening up to this other world and I know that if I persevere I'll see Craig again one day.

Amie offered me her manuscript to read and when I'd finished I came to realize that, firstly, 'Yay! I'm normal!' And I knew at once there'd be many other people who would find more than just hope in those pages.

Next, I learnt that I need to stop analysing everything and trying to get everyone else's opinions and acceptance. It's not their path. It's mine.

And I learnt that I need to slow down and be patient. The messages I'm getting are those that I need and am able to cope with at this time. It's not until your mind is open that you start to 'get it' and really acknowledge what's going on around you. It's not about working it out with your brain and this physical world. It's letting your mind accept. Then things start to happen.

When I was in my initial stages of grief I never thought it could ever get better, or that I could slowly learn to cope. But I do see now that while the pain is always there, we can begin to function with some kind of normalcy and get on with life.

I now see Amie as a person whose only motive is to genuinely help people, and I have a greater understanding of who she is. She has shown that even though she still carries the pain of losing her own son she is well able to offer me, and others like me, much-needed consolation and guidance.

* * *

As Catherine slowly emerges from the fog of pain I'm being treated to glimpses of her charming personality and delightful sense of humour, both of which I'm sure she felt would never again see the light of day.

Chapter 27

I look back over those years since 1982 with acceptance and appreciation of the life-changing lessons that have been presented to me. The journey would have been so much easier had I known from the beginning that life holds many secrets, but my internal spiritual alarm clock wasn't set for that time.

The earlier incidents, such as the signs I was given that Wayne would die, seeing him on St. Patrick's Day, the light-headedness and goose bumps at Brian's place, the 'awakening' during my first meditation, as well as other experiences – should have highlighted the simple fact of my extreme sensitivity to the energies around me. But they didn't. And consequently, instead of seeing those events as normal, I spent years looking for answers to a part of me that, in my mind, needed 'curing.'

Along the way I slowly uncovered fascinating jigsaw pieces that kept me wanting more and for these I'm so grateful. I now see the whole of existence through different eyes, even though I'm aware I've still scratched little more than the surface.

Spiritual sight has no boundaries and we are more than the magnificent creation that is our physical body. We do not die, and have each lived many lifetimes – not all of which have been on this earth – for we are immortal beings that change bodies like a new suit of clothing.

Everyone has the same potential for spiritual growth – or spiritual *remembering* – but it is almost impossible for those whose alarm clocks haven't yet gone off to relate to the wonder that is themselves.

Our guides and angels wait patiently for us to show some sign that we want to know what life is all about. There's a Universal Law that prevents them from interfering with our free will, but when at last they hear our questions, they can't help us quickly enough! Then a shift takes place in the laws surrounding our life and we become receptive to the energies that, though they always existed, were previously beyond our awareness. After that, we can never be the same.

But it is not my goal to convince people to see things as I see them, because there really are no words that will prove the profound truth of spiritual self-discovery. Instead, my aim is to help those who need validation of their experiences and to assure them that what is happening *to* them is right *for* them. All paths are different and there arc many ways to climb the same mountain.

www.ingramcontent.com/pod-product-compliance
Lightning Source LLC
Chambersburg PA
CBHW030755200726
48288CB00004B/1183